The Topaz Promise

THE
TOPAZ
PROMISE

Ruth Burnett

AVALON BOOKS
THOMAS BOUREGY AND COMPANY, INC.
22 EAST 60TH STREET ● NEW YORK 10022

The Topaz Promise

ONE

While Katherine Lonsdale sat at her desk in the living room of the apartment, the April sun came through the open window and turned her auburn hair into new-penny copper. She was frowning because she had apparently made a mistake on her income-tax return and could not seem to find it.

It was difficult to concentrate when the scent of lilacs came through the window and made her restless. It would be nice, she thought, to take a walk or go for a drive in the country. But the tax return had to be mailed by Monday and she was determined to finish it this afternoon, even if it was her birthday as well as Saturday and her day off from work at the dental office.

The old wooden clock ticked away from its place of honor on the mantel above the gas grate. That wooden clock was one of the few things that Katherine had brought with her when her parents died and their home was given up. She liked to hear it tick although many people said that ticking clocks made them nervous.

Katherine often thought that she herself did not have any nerves and she wondered what they were talking about. Anyway, she treasured the old clock. It had belonged to the Duvals, her mother's family, and she wouldn't part with it for anything.

In the center of the room eight-year-old Maggie had set up the card table and was putting a jigsaw puzzle together. Maggie loved jigsaws and had a stack of them almost as tall as she was. This was a new one that her Uncle Duval and Aunt Sarah had given her. And when it was completed, she said, she would have the whole United States. Maggie was having problems at the moment with the puzzle just as her big sister was having problems with her tax.

The telephone jangled.

"Answer the phone, please, Maggie."

Katherine had made some erasures and once again added a column of figures. She thought she had found her mistake and did not want to be interrupted by the telephone, so she paid little attention to Maggie's brief answers.

"Yes, sir.... No, sir.... Thank you, sir, but we're not interested." The child put down the receiver gently.

Maggie was a sophisticated miss for her eight years and knew how to deal with telephone solicitors. Katherine had taught her to be firm but polite.

After a while, Katherine got her figures straight and felt relieved, the way, she supposed, everybody felt when their tax return was finished.

Leaning back in her chair, she stretched her five-foot six-inch body, rubbed the back of her neck, and yawned. "I think I've got spring fever, Maggie. Who was that on the phone?"

"Just another giveaway. You know, they're always giving things away. Is Texas bigger than Alaska, Kick?"

Katherine's parents, while they lived, had always called her Kate, but Maggie had turned the name into Kick, so Kick it had remained for the child although Katherine would not let anybody else call her that.

"No. Alaska is bigger than Texas. It's the biggest state now. What were they giving away this time, Maggie? A million dollars or a trip to China?"

"No, not that. It was something about a log house in the mountains. The man talked funny and I couldn't understand him very well."

"You mean he was a foreigner?"

"I don't know. He just talked funny. Gee, isn't Ohio a little state? And look how small Indiana is. I thought they were big important states, but they're not near as big as the other states."

"Oh, we're not so little. There are other smaller states—little Rhode Island, for instance."

Katherine drew up her slim legs and sat up straight. Then she folded her tax return and sealed it in its envelope. It had been hard to stick to her desk today. One always likes to do something special Saturdays, particularly when it is also one's birthday.

Leaning back, she turned her hazel eyes toward her reflection in the mirror. Her short, wavy auburn hair looked neater than she'd expected, considering the way she'd been toiling with the figures. But Katherine did not realize just how lovely she looked.

Her beauty had come from her mountain mother and with it had also come a goodly portion of common sense and what her mother called gumption. Katherine was kind and considerate, self-reliant, and determined. She was also, as her Uncle Duval was fond of telling her, as stubborn as a porcupine.

She had not thought much about being twenty years old today until Maggie presented her with a handmade greeting card showing Father Time with his scythe. The child had also saved money from her small weekly allowance and bought her a red pen and pencil set.

Yesterday Katherine had received a beautiful needlepoint tote bag from Aunt Sarah, who, though an invalid, did fine handwork, and a comic card and a fifty-dollar bill from her uncle. Katherine had thanked them both profusely and submitted to twenty kisses and spanks from Maggie. She supposed she seemed very old to the child. When one is eight, twenty seems truly ancient.

"I can't even find Rhode Island," Maggie said as she shuffled through the puzzle pieces.

"Just go on looking. You'll find it," Katherine told her.

The clock on the mantel struck four and after that all was silent until the telephone rang again.

"I'll bet it's that giveaway man. You'd better talk to him, Kick."

"All right. I'll take care of him," Katherine said.

She got up from her chair, yawned again, and crossed the room. Picking up the receiver, she said hello.

"Is this Miss Katherine Elizabeth Lonsdale?"

"It is."

"My name is Conniston. Jacob Conniston. I'm calling from North Carolina. I tried to reach you a little while ago, but some child answered the phone."

"That was my sister who answered."

Maggie looked up from her puzzle. Katherine threw her a quick kiss and went on listening. The man did have a slight accent, but she recognized it immediately. It was a North Carolina accent.

"How old are you, Miss Katherine?"

She was so surprised at the question that she gasped into the mouthpiece, "Why, what on earth—"

He did not seem at all put out. "What I asked was how old you are," he said patiently, as though he were accustomed to talking with people who were slow of comprehension.

"Why, I'm twenty years old today. This is my birthday."

"Thought so. Congratulations."

"Thank you."

This weirdo actually seemed pleased

that she was twenty years old. Had he called from North Carolina to sell her something? She could make no sense of his words and yet it did not seem to be just a nuisance call. His drawl rather captivated her, too, so she waited instead of cutting him off.

"You think my question is rather silly, I know, but I just wanted to be sure that I had the right lady," he said agreeably. "As I told you, my name is Conniston. Jacob Conniston."

"Jacob?"

"Yes. I'm calling from Glen St. John in western North Carolina, and I'm an attorney."

Katherine's white forehead wrinkled in confusion and her eyes swept the room without seeing anything. An attorney?

"Are you sure you have the right number? I'm afraid I don't understand just what you want, sir."

"I'm getting to it. Your grandmother

was Mrs. Katherine Lonsdale who lived here in North Carolina. Right?"

"Yes, but I—I don't . . ."

Katherine still had her pen in her hand. She put it in her mouth and bit hard on it before she remembered that it was her gift from Maggie. Then she laid it down on the telephone stand.

"But my grandmother never—"

"I know. She did not acknowledge you as her granddaughter. That was because she did not like the woman who became your mother. Your father was John Henry Lonsdale and your mother, Maria Duval. That's correct, isn't it?"

"Yes, that's right."

"You see, I know about you. I wrote you a letter explaining all that I'm about to tell you now, but the letter was returned to me, so I've been trying to reach you by phone."

"Where did you send the letter, Mr. Conniston?"

"It was a number on Sheffield Avenue up there in Cincinnati."

"But I haven't lived on Sheffield Avenue for four years. Not since my parents died."

"I understand that now. The situation is this, Miss Katherine. Your grandmother, as you probably know, has been dead for several years. She bequested her home here in Glen St. John to her nine dogs, along with her cash, which was to care for them until they died. Did you know about that?"

"Yes. I remember my father reading about it in the paper and telling me. My grandmother was an unusual kind of person, Mr. Conniston, and you don't seem to understand that she refused to have anything to do with my parents or me."

"I know. She told me. Now, here's the rest of the story. Are you listening?"

"I'm listening, but there isn't any more to the story. That ended it so far as she was concerned."

"You're wrong. There is some more to the story. It's true that the house and the money were left to the dogs and they could never be moved from the house. When you were twenty, however, the house and the money would be yours."

"Mine!" Katherine gasped.

"Yes. By that time the dogs would all be dead and gone. They were all neutered, you know."

"No. How would I know?"

"Well, they were." His tone, which had been brisk and businesslike for a moment, returned to its slow drawl. "The problem is that the last stray dog your grandmother picked up—she told me she found the puppy under a laurel bush the same day that she got word of your birth and was told you were named for her. Anyway, that dog is still alive and is twenty years old, as you are. Since your grandmother's first consideration was her dogs, the house still legally belongs to that twenty-year-old dog and not to you, even if you are now twenty. Am I making myself clear, ma'am?"

"Well, I think so." Katherine was as doubtful as she sounded.

He went on talking, repeating some of what he had already said. When he finally paused, she thought she had the gist of it all. She had inherited her grandmother's house. But if she wanted the house, she would need to share it with an old pet as long as the pet lived.

That part was all right, Katherine told herself, because she was fond of all animals and particularly fond of dogs. But there were two big problems: the location and the money. The house was four or five hundred miles away from Cincinnati and the dog could not be moved. So Katherine would need to become the "keeper" of the dog herself or continue to hire the housekeeper who had been in charge of the house and dog since her grandmother's death. But because of the increasing cost of upkeep and help, of taxes and insurance, of dog

food and vet bills, the money was practically gone. What did Miss Katherine
want the attorney, Jacob Conniston, to
do about it?

Katherine's stomach fell with appre-
hension. She wished she knew more
about legal things.

"Do I—do I have to decide right now?"

"No. Not right now. Of course, when
the dog dies, you will be free to sell the
house. There is a summer visitor here
from Miami. His name is Page and he's
been coming to the Glen for many years.
He's very anxious to buy the house, but
until Sally Jo dies, the place is not yours
to sell."

"Sally Jo?"

"That's her name. The dog's name."

"I see."

"Now, Miss Katherine." The drawl
picked up speed and sharpened a bit.
"I've told you something of the situation. I'll try to make it clearer in a letter
which I'll get off today and you should

receive early next week. In the meantime, you should think about the matter—give it a really good think—and be ready to tell me what to do. If you can afford it, you may want to carry on the way we have been doing it."

"And how much would that cost?" That was really an unnecessary question because, no matter what it cost, she was sure she could not afford it. Still, she was not prepared for his answer.

"Well, altogether, counting utilities, food, housekeeper wages, vet bills, and everything, it will run about a thousand a month, which is quite reasonable considering everything. The house is in good repair, but you know that all houses need upkeep and this one will require a new roof in another year or two."

"A thousand a month!" Katherine was dumbfounded. "That much money just to keep a dog in a house!"

"Yes. It might even be a little more.

That's a guess on my part. I haven't examined the place for any needed repairs lately."

"But there's no way I can afford anything like that!"

"Well, now, think about it and see if there is any way you can afford *not* to continue the present arrangement. The instructions stipulate that if you refuse to accept the house, it will be given to the Humane Society. Your grandmother thought that you might refuse the gift because of the strained relations between her and your parents."

"No. I wouldn't refuse it for that reason. I just couldn't afford it, Mr. Conniston. Let's just give it to the society right now and let them take over the care of the dog. Just forget the whole thing."

"Now, wait a minute, Miss Katherine. That would mean that you would give up everything, so don't decide right now. Take a little time and, at least, wait for my letter."

"All right," she said reluctantly, "I'll wait for your letter, but I could not possibly afford to keep that house and the dog."

Katherine's mind was a chaos when she put down the receiver and walked, without feeling the floor under her feet, back to her desk and sat down.

Maggie looked up from her puzzle.

"I've found Rhode Island. What was that about a dog, Kick? Are they giving away dogs now?"

TWO

Turning a pencil end over end on her desk, Katherine tried to explain to Maggie what the man on the telephone had been talking about. The child looked puzzled and started to bite her fingernail.

"Don't do that," Katherine warned. "You know Aunt Sarah told you your nails would collect in your liver and kill you."

"I forgot." Maggie went back to her jigsaw puzzle.

19

The reason she could not explain what it was all about was that she was confused herself, Katherine decided. She should try not to think about it and just wait for the letter, but did Jacob Conniston know what he was talking about?

For a while she sat and stared at the income-tax envelope with a fixity of attention that had nothing to do with income tax. Then, mechanically, she took her purse from the bottom desk drawer, opened it, and removed a stamp that she put on the envelope. She could mail it when she and Maggie went out after a while for hamburgers, fries, and shakes. That was the way they celebrated special days like birthdays.

The golden sunlight had faded from the room and Maggie, looking out the window, said that it was getting late and dark, and she would need to hurry to finish her puzzle before it was time to go.

"It's not late," Katherine said. "It's just cloudy now and that's because it's

April. There's sun one minute and clouds the next."

April, she thought, could behave like June and then like February. The month was like an adolescent who puts away childish things one day and the next day goes and gets them out again. But Katherine liked April just because it was a month of surprises. There were never surprises in a midwest winter.

"Now I can't find West Virginia." Maggie shook her blond bob. "The big states are easy to find, but the little ones are hard."

"You'll find it. I. s there."

Katherine went back to thinking of the telephone call and Jacob Conniston and how he seemed to turn his hillbilly drawl off and on like a switch. She wished she could talk to her uncle about the call, but she couldn't. Not today. Although it was Saturday and Doctor Duval had no office hours on Saturday, he had gone to the hospital to work on an abscessed tooth for a man in an iron lung. Because he could only work two or three minutes at a time, it would be late when he got home. She would need to wait and tell him about the call later.

Her grandmother, for whom Katherine was named, had been a strange person. Everybody told Katherine that. While her parents lived, her father had done his best to be reconciled with the old lady but she would never answer his letters or talk to him on the telephone.

In her eyes, he had committed an unpardonable sin and insulted his family by marrying a Duval. Toward the end of her life, the old woman had been willling to let him come and see her, but he must not bring his wife. Duvals and Lonsdales had been enemies for generations in North Carolina, and no Duval would ever cross her threshold.

Katherine's father would never go to see his mother without his wife, and so they had never returned to the mountains but had lived in Cincinnati where her mother's brother, Doctor Sam Duval, was a dentist.

When Katherine's parents died in a tragic restaurant fire, it was not the grandmother down in the Carolina mountains who cared what became of sixteen-year-old Katherine and four-year-old Maggie. It was Doctor Duval who looked after them, who saw Katherine through her last year of high school and then through the dental hygiene courses.

When she was ready, he gave her a job in his office. Uncle Duval (he did not want to be called Uncle Sam) and his invalid wife, Sarah, helped Katherine find an apartment in a building near theirs. Later he helped her buy a small white car, a Citation.

Her uncle and aunt would have adopted little Maggie and brought her up as their own, but Katherine would not consider that for a moment. Neither would she listen to other people, some of them complete strangers, who wanted to adopt little Maggie.

"She's my sister and I'll take care of her. I'll manage."

At sixteen she had not known just how she would manage, but she knew that she would never give up Maggie for adoption, not even to Uncle Duval. She still remembered how she had felt when she returned from the cemetery that day and the future looked so very dark. But no matter what happened, she stubbornly told herself, she would keep small Maggie with her. And her loving uncle and aunt had decided to cooperate.

At first the going had been rough as Katherine took Maggie to kindergarten and brought her back each evening, as she doctored her colds and soothed her fears from bad dreams and storms, as she read her interminable stories and played games with her. And worked on puzzles! Maggie always adored puzzles—just any kind of a puzzle.

Everything was much easier now with Maggie in the third grade and liking school, head of her class, well adjusted, and taking part in everything. Katherine was as proud of Maggie as any mother could have been. The child had grown prettier every day with her very light blond hair and big velvety brown eyes, the same striking coloring their father had had.

Uncle Duval and Aunt Sarah seldom interefered with the care that Katherine gave Maggie, but on one subject they were adamant: Maggie must not keep Katherine from associating with other young people. They insisted that Katherine have dates and go to parties and dances and not devote herself exclusively to her sister, and they were always ready to take care of Maggie while Katherine enjoyed herself.

Katherine was popular. She laughed easily and she liked dancing. And there were three young men in her past that she'd been rather interested in.

First there was Sherman. She had gone to her senior prom with Sherman and dated him for almost a year after graduation. They got along well, never quarreled, but finally parted just good friends. Then there was Carl, but Katherine's attachment to Carl was rather unhappy from the beginning. When he kept insisting that other men got far more from their dates than he did, Katherine broke it off. She did not care *that* much for Carl.

With Mark Sinclair, though, things were different, for Katherine felt that she really loved Mark. They had talked of marriage, but Mark did not like Maggie. He did not like any children, he finally admitted, and never wanted any of his own. That was the end of that. Katherine would never give up Maggie and someday she wanted a family. Still, it hurt much more when she parted with Mark than it had hurt with the other two combined.

They were all three gone from her life now. Sherman had won a scholarship to UCLA and was studying genetics. Carl was making a career in the Air Force and was stationed in Las Vegas, while Mark, a journalist with a news service, was overseas.

In contrast, Katherine spent her days quietly, cleaning teeth or helping Uncle Duval mix fillings or calm a terrified patient. Or maybe she would even help Cleo, their secretary, catch up on her filing. There was certainly nothing romantic about her job, but she did have Maggie. And Maggie, she told herself, was worth it all.

"There it is, Kick! I've put the United States together when it was all in pieces. Isn't it lovely? Come and look."

Katherine came out of her reverie and walked over to inspect the puzzle.

"Yes, it's a beautiful big country, all right. Show me where you live."

Maggie pointed to Cincinnati. Then she found the largest state and the smallest state and many other places of interest.

Meanwhile, it had begun to thunder outside.

Katherine glanced through a window. "Just look how it's raining!" She dashed over and closed the windows quickly.

"Well, I thought we might walk for hamburgers, but now we'll need to drive."

"We could take an umbrella," Maggie said.

"It's too windy. We've only got one umbrella and this wind would ruin it. We'll drive."

Uncertain April! No wonder it was called the fickle month. At the moment Katherine felt as uncertain as April. What was she going to do about the house? Jacob Conniston did not seem to want her to give it to the Humane Society. But he just didn't understand that he was talking about the kind of money she simply didn't have. And yet he had said the decision was up to her.

What was he like, this North Carolina attorney? He sounded nice with that soft drawl. Jacob. Katherine thought of the Jacob in the Bible who saw the angels going up and down the ladder.

She remembered the old story vividly now although she had not thought of it for years. She wondered if this Jacob, too, dreamed dreams and saw visions.

Something told her that he did.

THREE

Three days later, Katherine, with Maggie beside her, was driving through the Great Smoky Mountains. She was heading for Glen St. John and her grandmother's house.

Maggie was impatient to reach their destination.

"We're going awfully slow," she said while they were eating their picnic lunch at the side of the road.

"I know, but we don't need to hurry through here. These mountains have been here for millions of years and it wouldn't be right to speed."

Indeed, it seemed rather indecent to Katherine to hurry through such scenery—with its ferns and blossoms, its woods and streams—and she was beginning to understand why her mother and father had said they would always miss the mountains. She had not understood before.

Katherine thought they would be near Glen St. John by dinnertime. But she planned to stop somewhere along the highway for dinner before she called the lawyer. Then they would be free to spend the night where he recommended, probably a motel.

But first she and Maggie had a whole afternoon before them, with more lovely vistas and blossoms and woods to admire.

At one point a forest ranger even showed Maggie a nearby bear and two cubs.

The child was enchanted by the baby bears.

"They're cute! So cute!" she exclaimed. "They look just like teddy bears!"

"They are cute," the ranger agreed, "but don't you ever try to pet one of them, young lady. They can claw you to ribbons!"

A few moments later, though, he let Maggie toss an apple to the bears from the safety of the car.

For the next few miles Maggie could talk of nothing but the bears.

"Just wait until I tell Uncle Duval that we saw a bear—a real bear in the woods with her babies!"

Katherine thought that Uncle Duval had likely seen dozens of bears, but she did not say anything to dampen her sister's enthusiasm.

As they drove along, Maggie kept looking for more bears while Katherine thought it was a kind of miracle that they were here in the mountains.

On Monday the letter had come from Jacob Conniston as he'd said it would. But although it was a long letter, it did not tell Katherine much that he had not already told her on the telephone.

When she showed the letter to her uncle, she admitted that she did not know much more about what was going on than she had known before.

Her uncle read the letter slowly, his bald head shining above his fringe of gray hair.

Then he said, "It all sounds unreasonable and quite complicated, and I'm afraid you can't look this gift horse in the mouth, Katherine. Don't get your hopes built up, though."

"I won't. You know I don't build cloud castles or have wild daydreams, Uncle Duval. I told this Jacob Conniston that we should just give the place to the Humane Society now and forget about it."

"No, no. That won't do either. You just can't make an important decision

like that on the spur of the moment.
You must know exactly what you're
doing. Now let me make a suggestion."

"What is it?" Katherine asked.

"Spring break for Maggie is this very
week and next Monday. I can let you
have the week off, too, Katherine. And
next Monday. The thing for you to do
is to go down to Glen St. John in North
Carolina and look the situation over
firsthand. I had no idea that your
grandmother would ever give you even
a chance at that house. It's really a fine
place, really unique. She designed it
herself when she was young and it's
more like a mountain lodge than just a
little log house."

There was nothing that Katherine
wanted more than to go to the mountains and see for herself, not just her
grandmother's house but that fabulous
mountain country she had heard so
much about. Yet she felt her trip would
be futile. There was no way she could
afford to keep that house.

"I'd dearly love to go, Uncle Duval, but—"

"Then go you will. Do you have the telephone number of that attorney?"

"It's there on the letterhead."

"So it is. Well, I'm going to call him immediately and tell him you're coming. Connistons have lived around Glen St. John for generations, and they have a reputation for honesty. Old Judge Conniston sat on the county bench down there for twenty-five or thirty years, but it's just as well that this man knows you have a male relative backing you. I don't want him to get the idea that you're helpless."

"Me—helpless? Why, you're always telling me not to be too independent and stubborn and—"

"Oh, hush. You know what I mean. You are stubborn and you can be downright bullheaded, but he might try to impose on you before he found that out."

Katherine did not argue the matter,

but she did not think that the voice on
the telephone or the tone of the letter
could belong to a man who would impose on anybody. Besides, she did not
consider herself defenseless at all.

Aunt Sarah, confined to her wheel-
chair for three years by a stroke, spoke
up.

"You must remember, Sam, that the
mountains and the people there are
likely a lot different today than when
you lived there."

"Maybe, but I doubt it."

Aunt Sarah smiled. "Sam used to
tease me all the time about his people
in the mountains. He said they were
barefoot, moonshining hillbillies who
kept a lot of hound dogs and lived on
squirrel stew and fish, which they covered with homemade ketchup."

"That's right," her husband assured
her solemnly.

"Nonsense! It would be entirely too
cold in the mountains to go barefoot."

Katherine laughed. "I'll soon find out

if they go barefoot, Aunt Sarah, and let you know."

Early Tuesday morning, she and Maggie got in the car and turned south.

Before she left, her uncle had given her detailed instructions about the route, and she was confident she would not get lost.

Uncle Duval had also told Katherine, "Now when you reach the Glen, you are to call Mr. Conniston and tell him you have arrived. I told him you would probably be calling between six and eight o'clock."

Everything had been exactly as Uncle Duval had said, only much more beautiful than he'd described it.

As the sun was getting lower in the sky, they reached a clean and attractive restaurant called The Mill Wheel and went in. Katherine guided Maggie to a rather secluded corner table. She did not want them to be conspicuous in a strange place.

Several people were already having

dinner although it was early. And
Katherine was surprised to see four
musicians already playing country and
western music.

The two girls ordered fried-chicken
dinners. Then, while they waited for the
food to come, they looked at quilts, pil-
lows, pottery, and all sorts of things at
the craft shop in back of the restaurant.

"Everything here is made by mountain people," the big woman in the craft
shop told them.

Maggie bought a little cornstalk doll
and they went back to their table. The
crisp chicken was delicious.

They were eating their cherry pie
when some of the diners began to dance.
It was mostly free-style dancing, with
people making up their own steps.

Maggie was fascinated.

"Look at those people! Isn't that girl
beautiful!" she exclaimed as a hand-
some man and exquisitely dressed girl
started dancing.

The two were looking at one another

in open admiration. Katherine had already noticed the couple. They certainly did not look like hillbillies, so they must be tourists, she decided.

"Look at her clothes, Kick!"

"Shh. Not so loud, Maggie."

"But aren't they pretty?"

"Very pretty."

The girl was tall and blond. Willowy tall. She wore a black skirt that was full enough to swirl and show her elegantly slim legs. Her blouse was exquisitely embroidered and seemed just perfect for this countryish place.

The girl would have been smart looking anywhere in the world, but here in the mountains she was especially striking.

The man, too, was attractive in a carefully tailored herringbone suit. He was tall and lean and perhaps, Katherine thought, about thirty years old.

When the couple was close to their table, the man smiled at Maggie and then his gray eyes met Katherine's hazel eyes and lit up with interest, while the corners of his mouth hinted at a smile. Then his partner said something to him and he turned to give her his undivided attention.

A little later, Katherine saw him glance at his watch and then say something to the blond girl, who nodded. They stopped dancing and almost immediately left the restaurant.

"Gee." Maggie rolled her eyes as she had seen eyes rolled on television. "Wasn't he some hunk of a man and wasn't she a beautiful woman! When I grow up, I'll find me a man like that. He seemed to like the way you looked, Kick."

Katherine ignored the remark and told herself for the hundredth time that she must not let Maggie watch so much TV.

But she had to agree with the child. He had been a fine-looking man and some magnetic impulse had made her eyes lock with his. She thought he had felt it, too.

Oh, well, she mused, don't start thinking about him. You'll probably never see him again.

To her consternation, however, Katherine was still thinking about the magnetic young man as she stopped for gas in the small town of Glen St. John.

Maggie, meanwhile, got into a conversation with the friendly gray-haired station attendant. Soon she was asking him to name some of the flowers on sale in front of the nearby supermarket and also some other flowers that she'd spotted around town.

When the gas tank was full, Katherine headed for the nearest phone booth, which happened to be in front of the post office. She dialed the number of Jacob Conniston's law office.

Immediately the pleasant voice drawled, "Hello. Are you here, ma'am?"

"Yes, I'm here," Katherine said.

"Did you have any trouble?"

"Not a bit. We had a good trip."

"Okay, then, Miss Katherine. You go right on up to your grandmother's big log house and I'll meet you there in twenty minutes."

"But I don't know where the house is."

"I'm about to tell you. Where you calling from?"

"From the front of the post office."

"All right. Now, you drive straight ahead until you come to the second road on your left. You'll have to climb then. Prepare to keep going. Don't stop. The road is asphalt, but it's narrow. When you get to the top of the mountain, the road ends and you're in the woods. You'll see the big log house on your right. Mrs. Taylor—or Miss Lizzie Taylor, as we say in these parts—is there and will let you in. She knows you're coming and has your room ready for you."

The climb was certainly steep. Maggie was scared and kept crying that the car was going off the mountain.

"Now look, you've got to keep still," Katherine scolded. "I can't stop and let you walk, so just hush."

The road leveled off near the top and they could finally laugh at their fears. Katherine turned to the right.

There was the house!

Her eyes took in the orange azaleas and other colorful flowers in every corner and cranny, the pines and hemlocks, the rustic bridge over the mountain stream. It was like a symphony.

And the house itself!

It was huge and beautiful. Its logs had mellowed to a soft beige and the cement caulking was turned by time to a deep ivory. There was a long one-story middle section, and on each side rose a two-story wing.

"Gosh," Maggie said, "it looks like a castle!"

"Well, not exactly," Katherine said.

"A hotel then."

What Katherine was thinking as they got out of the car and walked across the flagstone terrace was simply, And all of this for a dog!

Before she could lift the door knocker, the large plank door opened. Standing in front of them was an old woman and a big black-and-white mongrel dog.

FOUR

The floppy-eared, feisty-looking dog wagged her tail in greeting, and the housekeeper held out her hand.

"You're the new owner, aren't you? I heard your car and knew it was you. I'm Miss Lizzie Taylor and this is Sally Jo. Come right in and sit down."

Katherine took the old woman's hand. She noticed that Miss Lizzie had a warm smile and well-made, well-kept dentures. There was a natural dignity about her and even about the dog.

Katherine smiled into the raisin-like

eyes. She liked the housekeeper immediately.

"Thank you, Miss Lizzie. I'm Katherine Lonsdale and this is my sister, Maggie."

"I'm very pleased to know both of you, I'm sure. Come back here, Sally Jo!"

The dog, taking advantage of the open door, had gone outside and across the terrace. She paid no attention to the old woman's order to come back. Miss Lizzie clapped her hands loudly and the dog turned. At that the housekeeper motioned her to return, and Sally Jo trotted obediently back inside before the door was closed.

"She can't hear very well anymore," Miss Lizzie explained, "but she understands hand signals. I can't let her go outdoors without me because a car might hit her or a snake might get her. She just can't hear enough to keep out of danger. Did you have a good trip, and did you leave your people well?"

"Yes, thank you."

Katherine sat down on the long sofa in front of the fireplace. Flames leaped cheerfully up the chimney and were reflected in the copper kettle filled with logs that sat on the hearth.

"We saw a big bear and two baby bears," Maggie said.

"Did you now? About seven weeks ago one came right up to the door here."

Maggie's eyes widened. "It did! What did you do?"

"Well, he looked pretty hungry and I didn't have anything much in the house and bears like to eat, so I gave him a pan of Sally Jo's dog chow."

"Did he like that?" Maggie asked.

"Oh, yes. I watched him from that window right over there." She pointed to the large window that looked out over the terrace. "When he had polished off the chow, he tried to eat the pan. He had trouble chewing it, but he took it with him and I never did find the thing."

"Are there a lot of bears around here?" Maggie asked.

"Oh, no. They never wander over here except when there's so much snow that they can't find anything at all to eat."

"Do they ever hurt people?" the little girl asked.

"Gracious, no. We don't bother them and they go on back."

"Another thing we did," Maggie went on, "we stopped at the service station and the man there told us about all the little flowers in front of the supermarket."

"Did you now! That was my boy, Harrison, you talked to. Takes after my late husband. He's always been crazy about plants."

"Oh, no, it wasn't a boy. He was a man. He even had gray hair."

Miss Lizzie laughed, a good hearty laugh. "Yes, I know, he's getting gray, but he's my boy just the same. My oldest boy. He studied plants in college and gives lectures and shows pictures of plants. He even writes books about plants, and people are always bringing him things to identify."

"He didn't tell us anything like that," Katherine said.

"Oh, no, he wouldn't. He's not the kind who puts all his goods in the shop window."

Maggie looked puzzled at the remark and Katherine decided that mountain people were not like other people. But she certainly liked them. So far.

Sally Jo put her head in Katherine's lap to be petted. The dog's muzzle was gray. Her coat, however, was shiny. All in all, she seemed in good condition.

For some reason, Katherine had imagined that Sally Jo would be a lapdog, perhaps a poodle. Something small and aristocratic. She was glad to be confronted with a big, floppy-eared creature instead.

"She likes young'uns," the housekeeper said when the dog deserted Katherine for Maggie, who sat down on the floor with her. "She seems to prefer them to grown-up people. Have you had your supper yet?"

"Yes, we ate at a restaurant on the highway a while ago. I called Mr. Conniston and he said he'd be here soon."

"I know. He called me and told me. I can take you upstairs to your room now or wait until after his visit."

"Let's wait. I love the fire although I'm not actually cold at all. I just like to look at it."

"I do, too. I keep at least a little fire most all year round so the chimney won't ever get cold."

As she spoke, she put another small log on the fire, then took the hearth broom from its nail, swept the hearth, and hung the broom back up. "A clean hearth is a clean home."

How efficient the little woman seemed to be and how full of old sayings about clean hearths and shop windows she probably was!

Although Miss Lizzie was nearing

seventy, she was quite spritely. She told Katherine she had been a widow for ten years and had raised seven sons and one daughter. She bragged that there were more Taylors in the Glen now than there ever were Connistons, Lonsdales, or Duvals.

Katherine looked around her. She was already in love with the house: the raftered ceiling, the graceful twin stairways going up to the wings, the rustic light fixtures, the simple tables and chairs. All the wood was unpainted, the natural beauty of the grain giving it warmth and life.

Still looking around, Katherine was fascinated by the Indian masks on the walls and the colorful Indian rugs on the floor.

Although the large room contained a big piano, the stone fireplace was the center of attention. Above the mantel was an old portrait of a stern-faced man in some kind of uniform. He seemed about to draw his sword. Katherine's sister suddenly noticed the portrait, too.

"He looks mean," Maggie said. "Was he?"

"I don't know whether he was mean or not. I don't suppose he was," Miss Lizzie answered. "In those days men always tried to look mean like that for their pictures. He was General John Rutherford and he received all this land around the Glen for his services in the Revolutionary War. He was killed by a a Duval and that was what started the feud between the Lonsdales and the Duvals. I know you've heard about the feud."

Katherine said, "Yes, but I never knew what started it. That man wasn't any Lonsdale, though, Miss Lizzie."

"No, but when a man married into a family, then he always married the feud as well as the woman."

"Why did he kill him?" Maggie wanted to know.

"I can't tell you that. People always said different things, but most everybody thought it was a fair fight. Jake is coming now. I hear his car starting to climb the mountain."

Katherine could hear nothing. Miss Lizzie must have ears like a fox.

A moment later the housekeeper ushered Jacob Conniston into the room.

"Hello," he said.

Katherine gasped in surprise. He was the man she had seen dancing with the blond girl in the restaurant.

He laughed. "You know, I thought it might be you when I saw you in the restaurant. Your uncle told me on the telephone that you would have your eight-year-old sister, Maggie, with you."

Katherine felt her face warming. She thought he looked even more attractive now that he'd changed his jacket for a blue sweater.

"So you've already seen one another," Miss Lizzie said.

"Yes. I saw Miss Katherine well enough to know that she has the most beautiful eyes in the world."

With that he sat down on the sofa beside Katherine.

Miss Lizzie said, "You and your blarney! But I noticed Miss Katherine's eyes, too. They're Duval eyes. Don't let Sally Jo pull the threads in your sweater, Jake."

The dog had gone to him and put her paws on his knees. He patted her and playfully slapped her side.

"How are you, old girl? Did the vet stop by today, Miss Lizzie? I saw him at the post office."

"Yes, he was here and gave her a checkup, cut her claws, and looked at her teeth. He says she's the oldest dog in the state now. There's nothing the matter with Sally Jo except her ears and nobody can do anything about them. He thinks that, after living this long, she could last another five years."

"You're a celebrity now, Sally Jo," the lawyer said.

"Yes, she is." Miss Lizzie headed for the dining room on her right and the kitchen beyond it. "I'll go now and let you folks talk. I must give Sally Jo her supper. I always feed her by seven, then take her for a walk. We both go to bed at eight-thirty."

Katherine had not expected the lawyer to look like *this* and was still trying to think of something to say; when the housekeeper had left the room, she looked about and then turned to Jake Conniston.

"No TV for her to watch?"

He shook his head. "No. Our reception isn't very good in the mountains. I offered to bring Miss Lizzie an extra portable I had, but she didn't want it. She would rather go to bed and get up early. Mountain people like the fresh, clean mornings."

Maggie, who had not spoken since the lawyer walked in, found her tongue and began to ask questions. "That was a pretty lady you were dancing with at the restaurant, Mr. Conniston. Was she your wife?"

Katherine sent Maggie a warning look about asking personal questions.

He saw the look and smiled.

"I don't mind telling you. She's not my wife. Not yet. I'm not married. And please call me Jake."

"What's her name, Jake?" Maggie asked.

"Her name is Victoria. Victoria Page."

Katherine turned to look at the fire reflection in the copper kettle. A wave of something almost like disappointment passed over her because he'd said that Victoria was not yet his wife. Was she going to be his wife soon?

Katherine told herself she had no right to be jealous. It was none of her business.

Besides, Jake and Victoria Page did make an attractive couple.

He went on talking about the mountains and Maggie told him about the bear and her cubs and showed him the cornstalk doll she had bought. Then she

had to tell him that just seven weeks
ago a bear had come to the door right
here and Miss Lizzie fed him dog chow.

When Katherine could get a word in
edgewise, she asked Jake if he had always lived in Glen St. John.

"Oh, yes. My people bought land from
General Rutherford—that man up
there in the picture—and there have
been Connistons here ever since."

"But what do people do here for fun?"
Maggie wanted to know. "Do they go to
the movies?"

"Well, Maggie, they can go to the
movies if they want to, but a lot of them
go trout fishing and a lot of them are
rock hounds."

"Rock hounds? You mean some kind
of dogs?"

"No, I mean they go to the ruby
mines and dig for gems. Many of the
natives do that, too, but nearly all the
tourists and summer visitors are rock
hounds. We have a big Rock Hound Club
and I'm president."

Maggie was enthusiastic, but her sister just smiled.

"I didn't know this was gem country," Katherine said.

Jake said, "Oh, yes. At one time there were many mica mines, and mica was quite an industry. But it's given way now to plastics, like many other things. But we still have our ruby and sapphire mines."

"I'd love to dig. Can anybody dig who wants to?"

"Yes, Maggie. There's a small fee. You pay by the pail of dirt and sand you sift, but whatever you find of value is yours."

"I'd like to do that."

Jake said, "I'll tell you what, Maggie. Tomorrow morning I have a ten-o'clock meeting with the officers of the club at the Starlite mine for about an hour. I can take you along and you can dig while I discuss the club's business. Would you like that?"

"I'd love it! I'll bet I can find something, too, because I'm good at finding things. I found a ten-dollar bill last winter."

"Okay. Then if your sister approves, I'll pick you up about a quarter to ten and have you back here by noon."

"I don't mind," Katherine said.

"Good. Then, Maggie, wear your old clothes because you'll be digging in the dirt, you know. And take along a sweater in case you find the mine chilly. Be ready when I come for you because I mustn't be late for my meeting."

"She'll be ready," Katherine promised. "She'll probably be ready by daylight."

Jake turned back to Katherine. "I know you're wondering why I don't talk business, but I want you to have a chance to settle in and make yourself at home. We can talk business later. You see, I want you to like our mountains. We think our Glen is beautiful."

He reached over and patted her hand, and a warmth went creeping up Katherine's arm.

"I do like the mountains very much," she said, deliberately making her tone formal. "I can understand now why my parents loved them."

She was excitedly aware of his closeness and edged a little away from him just as Miss Lizzie came back into the room with a leash on the dog, ready for a walk. She wore a brown corduroy jacket over her dress and a fuzzy red cap on her head.

Maggie immediately wanted to know if she could go along.

"Of course, you can, but put something on over that thin shirt. It's getting cooler outside," her sister said.

Maggie obediently donned her sweater, chattering all the while.

"Jake is going to take me to the ruby mine tomorrow morning and let me dig for rubies while he has a meeting."

Miss Lizzie nodded. "He would. He's a real rock hound. That's what they call people who dig for rubies and other gems."

"I know now. I thought he meant dogs at first. Did Sally Jo have her supper?"

"Oh, yes. Sally Jo has always eaten like a team of horses. She likes everything. And Doctor Russell—that's the vet—thinks she should have cooked vital organs at least twice a week."

Katherine smiled at the mongrel and Sally Jo wagged her tail.

"She's a rock hound, too," Miss Lizzie said.

"You mean she'll go to the mine with us and dig?"

"No, not that. I mean that she collects rocks. You watch now and see if she doesn't bring a rock back in with her from her walk."

"What does she do with them?" Maggie asked.

"Over there in the corner, see that green chair? That's her chair and she piles the rocks in the corner behind the chair. When she gets too many, I take them outside again."

Maggie giggled and went quickly to

the chair to look behind it.

"She's got a lot there right now."

Katherine said she had never heard of a dog collecting rocks, but Jake nodded his head.

"That's right. According to the vet, it's not unusual at all. He says that nobody has ever been able to figure out why dogs do it, but many do collect rocks or other things."

Miss Lizzie said, "I just call it the pack rat in her. Everybody knows that pack rats collect things. All right, Sally Jo, we'll go."

The dog was jumping about and not liking the delay in her walk.

When they had left, Jake Conniston stood up.

"I'll go now, too, and I'll see you tomorrow. I'm sure you're tired after your trip and the excitement of a strange place, although I see it as a kind of homecoming for you, Katherine."

His gray gaze locked with her hazel one, but this time the contact was more comforting than challenging because she was tired.

"You've been a big help, Mr. Conniston." She stood up.

"Jake. Say it."

"You've been a big help, Jake."

"I'm a lawyer and it's my business as well as my pleasure to help people. You're really home folks, Katherine." He put his hands on her shoulders and looked at her seriously. "I can't tell you how glad I am that you came. See you tomorrow."

With that he was gone.

Katherine sat back down on the sofa and looked into the fire. She was warm—warmed by more than the heat of the flames. Jake was nice, she told herself rather primly. It was no wonder that Victoria Page had looked at him so adoringly as they danced.

FIVE

Just as he said he would, Jake came for Maggie shortly before ten in the morning, and she went running out to get into his gray Chrysler. Katherine went across the terrace, too.

"I'll bring you rubies and emeralds and pearls, Kick," Maggie promised.

"Not pearls, Maggie," Jake laughed. "Pearls grow in oysters."

"All right. I'll bring you just rubies then, Kick."

"Now don't count on finding anything, Maggie."

Katherine did not want the child to

67

be too hopeful. "Just have fun looking."

"Okay, I will."

Katherine watched them drive off and then went upstairs to straighten out the big room she was sharing with Maggie. The lovely old furniture appealed to Katherine. Flowers were painted on the headboards of the two beds and on the bureau and dresser. Everything about the comfortable room, including the old prints and photos on the wall, exuded a mellow air of history.

But the big adjoining bathroom was completely modern, as was the kitchen downstairs. Katherine had admired the kitchen while she and Maggie were having breakfast.

Miss Lizzie said it was a wonderful kitchen to work in. Then she told Katherine she had not been to her own home for a week. And if it was all right with Katherine, she would like to go to her house down the mountain long enough to get a few things and to pick up her mail. Her daughter told her over the phone that she had mail.

"Of course, Miss Lizzi, go right ahead. I'll be all right and I'll walk Sally Jo. Don't you want me to drive you?"

"No, I'd rather walk."

"But you'll have to climb back up the mountain."

"That's all right. I can climb these mountains better than any goat."

"I'll just bet you can," Katherine laughed.

"There's plenty of food in the refrigerator if you get hungry before I get back."

"All right. I'll clean up the breakfast things and you can get started."

Back in the living room after her voluntary chores, Katherine noticed that the copper kettle had been refilled with logs and she put another on the fire, remembering to sweep the hearth with the little broom. She could not resist the leaping flames.

After standing a while and looking at the fire, she took a tour of the house, becoming more and more enchanted with it.

Then she came back to the living room and sat on the sofa to watch the fire again.

Wouldn't it be nice to sit in front of the flames on a cold winter night and listen to the wind howl around the mountains? she thought. Maybe—just maybe—with Jake beside her on the sofa as he had been yesterday.

Daydreams. Foolish daydreams.

Suddenly, there was a knock on the door. Katherine jumped. Company? And she in faded jeans and T-shirt and her hair all mussed!

She got up and opened the door. A big man of about sixty stood there, and beside him—Katherine recognized her instantly—was the girl who had been dancing with Jake Conniston, Victoria Page.

"Good morning," the man said rather pompously. "I am Montgomery Page and this is my daughter, Victoria. May we come in?"

"Of course." Katherine opened the door wider. "Please come in. I am Katherine Lonsdale."

She took the hand he held out and the Pages both sat down on the sofa while Katherine took a chair nearby.

He was a big man with heavy jowls and bright blue eyes. Dressed immaculately in a carefully tailored gray suit, he looked the successful automobile dealer that he was. Victoria wore designer jeans and a white sweater. Her slim figure was superb and her blond hair glistened.

"We are your neighbors." Mr. Page smiled. "We live on the neighboring mountaintop. You must go down, across a bridge, and back up again to get to us. I understand that you are now the owner of this house."

Katherine nodded. "Yes, I am."

"I just wanted to drop by and get acquainted and to tell you that I'm interested in buying the place. Frankly, I have always liked it and I would like to be considered first when you put a price on it and start looking for a buyer, Miss Lonsdale."

"But I haven't really thought of selling, Mr. Page."

He nodded understandingly and his jowls shook.

"No, I suppose not. One can't do everything at once. Of course, you would have no use for such a big place. I understand you live and work in Cincinnati."

"Yes, that's right."

"You would not want it personally, I'm sure."

How could he be so sure? He went on talking about how he had been born and brought up in New Orleans but had been in business in Miami for thirty years, spending his summers in the mountains. Chestnut-log houses like hers were very rare, he said, and he had come up to the mountains early this year because he understood there was to be some action on this house.

"Of course, many people would not want a log house at any price, but I happen to like them and so does my daughter. I promised her I would buy this one for her someday, didn't I, honey?"

"Yes, Daddy, you did." Victoria kissed his cheek.

He went on: "Is this your first trip to the Glen, Miss Lonsdale?"

"Yes, it is. Did you know my grandmother, Mr. Page?"

He shrugged his impeccable gray shoulders. "I met her once or twice. That's all. But I do know Miss Lizzie Taylor and the whole Taylor family. They—at least some of them—have often worked for us, and they are excellent workmen. Do you like these mountains, Miss Lonsdale?"

"Yes, I do. I like them very much indeed."

"But you could never endure the winters here."

"Couldn't I?" Katherine asked.

"Oh, no. They're very bitter and the wind is so strong and cold, it blows you off the mountaintop if you try to take a walk."

"It's probably lonely, too," Katherine said, "especially when all the summer people are gone."

Victoria laughed, but her small blue eyes were cold. "Yes, it's lonely and desolate, and the nights are long and dark. No street lights, you know."

Were they trying to discourage her from living here in the Glen? If they were, Katherine thought they were crude about it.

Mr. Page began to talk about the bears that often came out of the woods.

"They can be a nuisance. People are afraid to let their children out of the house."

Katherine nodded. She was not going to argue that matter with them.

They did not stay and talk much longer. Mr. Page thanked her for talking to him and said he only wanted to make himself known and to make sure he'd be considered for the house when she was ready to sell it.

She could only tell him that she would not forget but that she had no plans until she learned a little more about things herself.

He made a polite departure while Victoria lingered.

When her father was out of hearing, she asked coldly: "How long do you expect to stay here?"

Surprised at the question and at the tone of her voice, Katherine only said, "Well, I'm not sure. There is business to attend to. Why do you ask?"

"I just wondered. You don't fit here very well and I didn't think you would stay long."

Katherine's eyes were disturbed.

"You sound as if you don't want me to stay."

"I don't. You're taking up too much of my Jake's time."

Her Jake. Of course.

"Well, I'm sorry. It's business, you know."

"It isn't business at all. You Yankees are all alike and—"

"I'm not a Yankee. I'm a midwesterner."

"It's all the same. You'll hook him like a trout if you can. But you can't, and you'd better believe it."

Victoria turned and left without another word.

Katherine closed the door and sat down hard on the sofa. She was surprised and angry. She was also provoked with herself because she had not been able to think of the right thing to say.

She was still sitting there, looking into the fire and thinking of all that she should have said, when Jake came back with Maggie. The child carried a bag of rocks.

"I didn't find anything good," she admitted quickly, "and neither did three old ladies who were digging with me, but I learned a lot about rocks. Jake says none of these are valuable, but I know the names of them now."

She put the rocks on the floor and sat down to sort them. When the dog came quickly to investigate, Maggie shoved her away.

"Oh, no, Sally Jo. You don't get any of mine. You've got your own rocks. Go play with yours."

"Can't you give her one?" Katherine asked.

"No. These are special. They're mine. We're going back to dig some more while I'm here."

"Are you?"

"Yes. Jake says so and the next time we're going to take you with us."

"Oh, I'm not lucky. I never found anything or won anything in my life. I have to do things the hard way."

Katherine sat down on the sofa while Jake took the big lounger chair and stretched out his long legs.

"You've got to go and try anyway," Maggie insisted. "It's fun to dig. Look at my hands."

"I've been looking at them. They're pretty dirty."

"Well, these rocks are very dirty things."

Katherine turned to Jake. "Mr. Page and his daughter were here a while ago."

He seemed surprised and lifted his head from the back of the chair.

"They were? Wanting to buy the house, were they?"

"Well, yes, wanting to be considered as prospects at least."

"That figures. He has always wanted the place. What did you tell them?"

Katherine shrugged. "I—well, there wasn't much of anything I could tell them. I just said that nothing had been decided as yet. He was very courteous about it."

"Oh, yes, Monty's a good business-man and would try hard not to appear too anxious, but he has always wanted to get his hands on this house."

"He admitted he did."

"Victoria likes it, too," Jake said.

Katherine nodded. She did not want to talk about Victoria.

The gray of his eyes acquired a kind of transparency as he looked at her. "Perhaps we had better start talking about the house. You've had time to look about and know more now of what your grandmother had in mind."

Katherine made a quick gesture of denial.

"I've looked about, all right, but I don't think I ever would know what my grandmother had in mind."

He looked at his watch and got up.

"I suppose not. Well, look, Katherine, your grandmother's will and a packet of papers which she considered important are in the safe in my office. My father always kept them for her. I have appointments this afternoon until four o'clock, but I'll be free from then on. If you'll drive to the office—it's right down on the highway, a one-story brick building near the post office—I'll get out the papers and we can go over the will together, anyway."

She felt relieved. "Good. I'd like that. I'd like to see the will."

He left a little later after answering a few more questions about rocks from Maggie.

Katherine was glad that Jake was ready to talk business. After all, she had come down here on business. Yet every moment since she had arrived, her mind had been a chaos of dogs and logs and bears and ruby mines and gray eyes in a lean male face.

SIX

That afternoon Katherine put on a blue dress and prepared to go to the law office.

Maggie said she would stay at home with Miss Lizzie, and Katherine was pleased that she did not want to go, for she would be sure to ask too many questions.

Katherine found the one-story brick building at once. A white-haired woman sat behind the reception desk. She smiled at the newcomer.

When Katherine gave her name, the woman's pleasant smile widened.

"Oh, you're Katherine! I'm Sondra Lonsdale and you're my third cousin once removed!"

She stood up quickly and held out her hand. Katherine took the hand with surprise and delight. It was a firm, strong handclasp.

"I didn't know I had a third cousin. I understood that the Lonsdale family had died out."

"That's right. It's pretty nearly gone." Sondra Lonsdale nodded. "But I'm left and so are you and your sister. I've been waiting to meet you ever since I heard you were coming. I knew your father and mother."

"Did you?"

"Yes, but not very well."

"And do you know all about the old family feud?" Katherine asked.

"Well, it's just a story to me. I love all the Duvals I know. They're fine people. Jacob has been telling me about you and Maggie," Sondra went on as she glanced at the big round clock on the wall. "But I mustn't keep you now. The school board is coming to see him later and you'll want time to talk. The board decided that they had to see him today."

"Thank you, Sondra. I do want to talk more to you. I'm glad I have a Lonsdale cousin and I want to ask you a lot of questions about my parents and grand-parents."

Sondra nodded and pointed to the door on the side. "You can go in now. He has a caller, but just a social caller, and he said to have you come right in."

Katherine walked into a book-lined office a little larger than the waiting room. There was a very big desk and a table with a computer.

Katherine did not really see the books, the desk, or the computer. What she saw was Jake at the desk and, standing behind him, Victoria Page with her arms about his neck, leaning over with her cheek against his.

When she saw Katherine, Victoria raised her head and smiled but kept her arms around Jake's neck possessively.

Jake loosened the arms and stood up. "Do sit down, Katherine. You're right on time. Run along, Victoria. I'll see you later."

"Okay." The blonde pouted and cast a disdainful look at Katherine. "You're the Lonsdale girl, aren't you?"

"Yes, I am."

"Excuse me," Jake said. "I thought you two had met. Miss Lonsdale, this is Miss Page."

Victoria was putting on an act and Katherine decided that she could act, too, so she said, "How-do-you-do?" and held out her hand.

For a second she thought that Victoria would refuse it, but she took it in a loose, cool clasp.

"I'm not sure," Victoria said in a dull tone. "Perhaps we have met. Well, I'll see you tonight, Jake. Don't forget that dinner is at seven and Dad is anxious to talk to you." She leaned over and kissed his cheek.

When the door had closed behind her, Jake indicated the chair at the desk opposite his.

"If you'll sit here, Katherine, you can see the papers better. By the way, is Maggie getting her rocks arranged?"

Katherine's smile was a little weak, but her heart, which had leaped into her throat at the sight of Victoria, had settled back down in her chest.

"Yes, Maggie's been spending a lot of time with those rocks. You've been very kind to her, Jake."

He leaned over to open a desk drawer and take out a manila folder.

"I like Maggie. She's my kind of girl and so is her sister."

Katherine let that pass and he immediately became a businesslike lawyer.

Taking some papers from the manila folder, he said:

"Here is your grandmother's will. My father drew it up and he was very good with wills. It's legal and airtight. She was very certain what she wanted done and my father felt that people had a right to leave their property as they chose to leave it. Your grandmother's dogs had become very important to her."

"Yes, I know."

"That isn't at all unusual. Many older people are very fond of their animals. Sometimes I think it's because they've lost faith in their fellowmen."

Katherine was now looking at the books on the shelves behind him. There were the usual law books and many other volumes. There were books on philosophy and history. There was poetry and great fiction. Some of the volumes looked very old.

Turning away from the books, Katherine began to read the will. It was short with no wasted words. It said the house must not be sold or mortgaged until the last of the dogs had died. Then it was to become the property, when she was twenty, of Katherine Elizabeth Lonsdale. In the event that she did not want the house, it was to be given, contents intact, to the Humane Society.

Jake said, "Now, Katherine, you can see that she doesn't say that you, yourself, cannot sell the house. But she thought you wouldn't take it in the first place. She told me once that you would likely be a stubborn bullheaded Lonsdale who would not accept anything that belonged to her because of the strained family relationship but that she would really like you to have the house."

"My grandmother said that! She said that she would like me to have the house?"

"Yes, she did. She had no reason to dislike you, Katherine. You hadn't disobeyed her. And I think she was pleased that, in spite of everything, your parents named you for her."

"What was my grandmother like, Jake?" Katherine asked.

"She was a strong-minded woman," he said. "And in her later years she never came down the mountain. But she was friends with the birds and wild creatures. She told me once she couldn't understand how anyone could be lonely when the world was so full of living things.

"When she wanted to see people, she had a way of ordering them up to the house. She did it with my dad or me. And Doctor Russell, the vet, says the same thing. She surely knew her own mind. And when she said she'd like you to have the house, she meant it. To keep or sell or do whatever you want with it."

"But I can't really have it as long as Sally Jo is alive."

"That's right. Sally Jo has first call on everything. Your grandmother had it all completely worked out."

"Except a way for me to pay all the bills."

Jake sighed. "She had no way of

knowing Sally Jo would live so long.
And she had no idea, any more than the
rest of us did, what was going to happen
to our economy. She thought she had
enough money to care for the dogs, but
Sally Jo has lived a very long time."

Jake took out some additional papers
and showed them to Katherine.

"These are yours since there is nobody else except Maggie who has a claim
to them. They're personal family mo-
mentos—old letters, marriage certifi-
cates, and so forth—some of them going
way way back. You take your copy of
the will and the other papers back to
the house with you and look at them
tonight while you're trying to decide
what to do. Later, I'll put those family
papers back in the safe and lock them
up for you if you want me to."

"I'll probably want you to do that."

The intercom began to buzz and Sondra said that the school-board members
were beginning to arrive. Katherine got
up.

Jake opened the door for her. "I'll see you tomorrow. How about in the afternoon?"

"Fine. I'll be at the house all day."

"Tell Maggie I'm going to give her the rock collection I had when I was in the third grade."

"Thank you," Katherine said, smiling.

Jake was standing very close to her and squeezed her hands.

"Don't worry, Katherine. Everything will be all right. I know that decisions like these are difficult to make, but you'll decide what to do."

Hugging the papers to her, she went out and got in the car. Turning the ignition key, she wished she had never come to North Carolina, wished she had never seen the house. For she wanted it very much and she could not keep it.

One thing was sure, Katherine told herself vehemently. She would donate the house to the Humane Society or to almost any other organization that

could take it over before she would let
the Pages have it.

Victoria Page was *never* going to get
the chestnut-log house.

SEVEN

Maggie was delighted with the rock collection Jake brought her the next afternoon shortly after lunch. And she was eager to join him and her sister in a drive around the countryside.

Jake pointed out gem mines, trout streams, and other spots of interest. He also related some fanciful local Indian legends.

Katherine's brain and heart were filled with turmoil. Each hour she spent in the house and each mile she traveled about the surrounding countryside made the thought of giving it all up hurt more and more.

Jake and Katherine were back in front of the fireplace now and the dilemma was making her irritable.

"Since you're a lawyer, Jake, you should be able to think of a way out of my predicament," she said bluntly. "Help me to keep this lovely house!"

"Oh, should I? Well, Katherine, as you say, I'm a lawyer, but that doesn't make me a magician. Besides, I'm legally the dog's lawyer and not yours. My father was hired years ago to look after the welfare of the dogs and not your welfare. I took over from my father and it's my duty to look after Sally Jo."

Katherine said, "I understand. My grandmother wasn't the least bit interested in my welfare." She looked at him with petulant eyes. "Somehow I thought that you would be."

Sitting in the big chair, his legs stretched out in front of him, Jake stared at her as though he had not quite heard her. Then he turned back to the fire without speaking.

Katherine realized that her words had gone too far and that he was disappointed in her. A smile took the place of her petulant expression.

"I shouldn't have said that. I'm ashamed of it, Jake. There was no reason why my grandmother should have been interested in me. She didn't know me. She loved her dogs and wanted them cared for, and I admire her for that. And I certainly shouldn't expect you to take on my problems. You've already been more kind and considerate than I had any right to expect."

Jake smiled, too.

"You know, Katherine, I really like you. You're stubborn like your grandmother, and I'll bet you could really bear a grudge, too, but I think you'd try to play fair when possible. You'll make up your mind about the house and do the right thing, I'm sure."

"I think I have made up my mind,

Jake." Her sudden frown was almost ferocious.

"All right, let's hear it."

He sat silent, waiting for the words to come.

"Well, I want the house. I told you that," she began in a hesitant voice. "I'll be sorry for the rest of my life that I had a chance to own it and just could not take advantage of the chance."

"But your uncle is a dentist and maybe he could—"

"No! That's not the way it's going to be. He's already done far more than he should have done for Maggie and me when he has a sick wife to care for. I won't take another dime from my uncle even to get the house!" Trying then to tone down her vehemence, she added softly, "And I do love the house."

"Who wouldn't?" Jake said.

His casual shrug and his tone antagonized her.

"You're being hard-boiled, Jake."

Now there was real irony in his voice.

"I don't think I'm being hard-boiled at all. You've got to remember that you've lived without this house for twenty years. Why should I get all steamed up and sentimental now because you suddenly decide that you want the house while at the same time you keep saying over and over that you can't afford it?"

"I can't," Katherine said.

"All right then. I can only tell you what you can and can't do legally. The logical thing would be for you to get a loan to carry you until the dog dies when the house would be yours. At least then you could sell it. But that, of course, wouldn't help if you wanted to stay here and couldn't afford it. Would you want to live here, Katherine?"

She nodded miserably. "I love this country and so does Maggie. I never dreamed I would fall in love with the house and the mountains the way I have. It was an awful mistake for us to come down here."

"Don't say that."

Jake came over to sit on the sofa beside her.

"Listen, Katherine." The drawl came back into his voice. "All of us want things we can't have. You'll get over it. I remember that I once wanted a motorcycle—a red-and-white Yamaha—but I couldn't have it. And by the time I could afford the thing, I didn't want it. It was the same with a Porsche I had set my heart on, but I finally settled for a secondhand green Chevy."

Katherine said, "What you're telling me is that I had better grow up."

"Something of the sort."

"Well, Jake, I'm telling you that I am grown up. This is not an adolescent notion of mine at all. I truly want to own the house, but on my salary as a dental assistant, and with a little sister to care for and educate, I cannot possibly take on the place with its taxes and upkeep and insurance and everything."

Taking her hand, he said, "Nobody can tell another person how to run his affairs. Even if I were a financial counselor, I wouldn't know the way out of your dilemma without more cooperation on your part."

"Cooperation! How can I cooperate? If I can't borrow the money, I just can't. And if I can't afford to keep such a place, I just can't. The only thing to do is to give it to the Humane Society right now. They may turn it into an animal refuge and my grandmother would like that."

He shook his head. "I don't call that any solution because I'm sure you need the money more than the society does if you're to see Maggie through school. If you let them have it now, you won't realize a nickel and I think you're entitled to something. If you wait till it's completely yours, you could sell it for a good price. You'll have to face facts, Katherine."

Face facts! All she had done since she first heard of the house in the mountains was to face the facts, and what good did it do? No matter how hard she faced them, they stayed there and stared back at her. She said nothing.

"Now I see one way that would keep you from losing everything, Katherine, but you'd have to part with the house. I don't suppose that you would accept a loan from me if I could manage to swing one?"

"No, Jake, that's sweet of you, but I wouldn't do that at all."

"Well, I thought of this: Mr. Page is very anxious to buy the house. He's never made a secret of it."

"But the house can't be sold until—"

"I know it can't. Not in an ordinary sale. But he's a rich man and I might be able to get him to make a substantial payment to you now if you would sign an agreement to sell him the house when the dog dies. No deed would exchange hands now. It's only an idea and I haven't broached the subject to Mr. Page at all."

"Oh, I wouldn't do that! I just couldn't!"

The thought of Victoria living in this house and Jake coming to see her here made the blood pulsate so violently in Katherine's veins that it brought on a fit of coughing. Jake hurried to the kitchen and brought back a glass of water.

"Are you all right, Katherine?" he asked.

"Yes." She smiled over the glass as she sipped the water. "It's just that I should never have come because Maggie and I were satisfied up there and—"

"By the way, where is Maggie?"

"She went to take Sally Jo for a walk. She said she was going to pick enough flowers for a bouquet for the window, and I expect that's why it's taking her so long."

Jake looked concerned.

"Well, Sally Jo knows her way around, but I wouldn't trust Maggie in these mountains alone if I were you. Now we're not going to talk any more about the house for a while. You can think about what I've said. I want to take you to dinner soon. We have a nice restaurant over in Highlands and the little theater group there is putting on *The Music Man*."

"I love that musical."

"Then let me see what I can do about tickets. Maybe we can go to dinner Saturday night or even tomorrow night and see the musical after dinner. You do like to dance, don't you?"

Katherine recalled the way Jake and Victoria had danced and hesitated.

"I like to dance, but I don't dance very often of late. You see, I've been busy working at the office and then, with Maggie—"

"I know. You've been cleaning teeth and mixing fillings for teeth."

"Yes, I have, but I wasn't thinking about teeth. I was thinking that I didn't bring any clothes to go dancing in. And that's the silly truth."

"Is that all? Well, that plaid skirt and

white blouse you had on the first time I saw you at The Mill Wheel Restaurant will do very well or the blue dress you wore to my office. You looked lovely in both of them."

So he had noticed! She glanced down at her jeans.

"Jeans won't do?" She smiled.

"No. The rule is no jeans or shorts where we're going. I want to show you one of our best places, but it is conservative."

"I'd love to go, Jake." Her eyes were bright at the thought.

At that moment Miss Lizzie came in from the kitchen. She wore her apron and was wiping her hands on a towel.

"Isn't Maggie back yet?"

She had scarcely asked the question before there was a scratching on the door.

Jake opened the door quickly and Sally Jo came in, dragging her leash.

The three looked at the dog and waited. Maggie did not come.

Miss Lizzie exclaimed: "Oh, my, where's that child?"

Jake hurried across the terrace and out to the drive, calling: "Maggie! Maggie!"

Katherine followed, but Maggie was nowhere in sight.

At first Katherine was not worried, but then, as she looked into the impenetrable forest, panic hit her and her heart began a wild flutter.

Maggie was lost!

EIGHT

Katherine stumbled across the terrace after Jake.

"Maggie! Maggie! Where are you!" she called frantically and then began to cry. "Oh, Jake, she's lost! I know she's lost! You go that way and I'll go this way!"

She headed into a laurel thicket and he snatched her arm.

"You'll do nothing of the sort! You either go back into the house and stay there or keep right behind me. I don't want both of you lost in these mountains."

"Wait!" Miss Lizzie called.

She had donned her corduroy jacket

105

and her red cap and held a sweater out to Katherine. She also had the dog on a leash and held the leash out to Jake.

"Take Sally Jo with you. She might help. Now, Jake, if you'll bear to the east, I'll take the west."

"Fine, Miss Lizzie. We'll take the old trail and search for just one hour—until five o'clock. If we don't find her by then, we'll come back and call the rescue squad."

The rescue squad! The words struck more terror into Katherine.

She was swiping at her tears and trying to keep up with his long legs. "Oh, Jake, we've just got to find her! It'll soon be dark and she's alone!"

"Maggie!" Katherine screamed. "Maggie!"

"You keep still, Katherine, and let me do the talking. Just follow me now and keep quiet."

Jake hurried on, pausing every little while to whistle loudly and to shout the child's name. All that he got in answer was an echo, a cruel, mocking echo. He seemed to be trying to let the dog decide which way to go when a squirrel ran across the path in front of them and Sally Jo made a break for it. The leash slipped from Jake's fingers, and the dog disappeared into the laurel.

"Oh!" Katherine wailed. "Now we've lost the dog! What are we going to do?"

He turned around and very unceremoniously told her, "Don't you say another word!"

The rebuke was just what Katherine needed. She sniffled and swallowed her sobs but from that moment began to gain control.

Dragging her by the hand, Jake plunged into the laurel thicket. On the other side, Sally Jo was climbing a steep incline. When she caught her leash in some brush and stopped, Jake grabbed the leash and held it tightly.

"Can't you walk any faster?" he demanded, forgetting that he had told her not to talk.

"No, but I can run."

"Run, then. I think she may have fallen into the mica mine and I want to hurry."

"Mica mine?" Katherine was chalk white and trembling. "Will she—will she be dead?"

Seeing her face, Jake became compassionate and put his arms about her for a moment.

"Of course, she won't be dead. She'll be all right. It isn't any more than a ditch. Come on, now."

It was hard walking with tangled briars and thick, tree-high laurel. When they reached a kind of clearing, Jake began to shout again.

"Maggie! Maggie! Where are you?"

"Here! I'm here!" came the child's voice.

Katherine stopped in her tracks. "I heard her!" She went limp with relief.

"We're coming, Maggie!" Jake called. "I know where you are."

Then, putting his arm about Kath-

erine's waist, he half carried, half
dragged her forward.

A few more minutes and they were
looking down into a thirty-foot-deep
trenchlike opening. They could see
Maggie's dim, small figure and they
heard her laugh.

"Maggie!" Katherine cried. "Are you
laughing?"

"Sure. Here I am! Right here! I can
see you. Can't you see me? I slipped and
slid down the sand, but Sally Jo didn't.
And now I can't get out."

"I'm coming for you," Jake called. "I'll
get you out." Then he turned to Katherine. "Can I trust you to stay right
here and not move from this spot until
I come back?"

She smiled wanly. "Oh, Jake, I'm
sorry I've been more trouble than Maggie. But you can trust me. I'll stay right
here."

"I must take her around about a
quarter of a mile where there's a kind
of ramp, and I've got to know that you'll

stay here and not move until I get back with her. It's going to take me a while if the sand has caved in. You hold on to the dog."

"I'll wait," Katherine promised, "right here by this tree."

Grabbing a thick vine, Jake lowered himself hand under hand to the bottom. Looking down, Katherine saw the two of them dimly as they moved out of sight.

She leaned against the tree and drew her sweater about her. Sally Jo sat quietly against her leg. Although the worst was over, Katherine still felt shaky.

It seemed like hours before she heard Jake and Maggie's voices and saw them coming, like shadows, toward her. She tried hard to hold back the tears as she hugged the calm child, who was not frightened at all.

"Why, I knew you'd find me," Maggie said in surprise. "You shouldn't have been worried, Kick. Of course, if Sally Jo had fallen in with me, she might have known the way out. But, anyway, Jake knew how to get out."

"But didn't it hurt when you fell so far?" Katherine asked.

"No. It was just like a long, sandy slide. It didn't hurt, but I did get a little dirty."

Maggie still clutched a handful of violets and wild iris, and she and Jake chattered all the way back to the house.

"Why, Sally Jo knew where I was and I knew you'd find me. It wasn't that I was lost. I just couldn't get out, that was all. I don't believe I would ever get really lost because I have a good bump of locality."

Jake was amused at that remark, but Katherine could not feel amused at any of it.

At the house Maggie and Jake took off their shoes, emptied out the sand, and put them back on again. Then they washed up and told Miss Lizzie all about it.

Miss Lizzie said she had talked to two

of her boys—the two who were on the rescue squad—and told them to be ready in case they were needed. Now she called them back to tell them that Maggie had been found.

"Stay for supper, Jake. We have vegetable stew and fresh hot bread," the housekeeper invited, but Jake shook his head.

"I'd love to, Miss Lizzie, but I have a man coming to see me at seven. It's that Mr. Coggins who had the car wreck. You know him."

"Yes. He still says, though, that if he hadn't had his seat belt fastened, he could have jumped before he went over the side of the mountain."

Katherine listened, thinking that it had never occurred to her that rules that were good for flat country might not be good in the mountains. Mountain country had laws and rules unto itself.

Maggie reminded Jake that they were to go back to the ruby mine.

"I haven't forgotten, Maggie, but I'll

have to let you know when I can go.
Maybe tomorrow. We'll see."

Long after Maggie and Miss Lizzie
and Sally Jo were asleep, Katherine lay
thinking. She had loved Maggie from
the moment her parents had put the
little red mite in her arms and told her
it was her baby sister. When their parents died, Katherine's love had inten-
sified, but she had not really known how
dear the child was to her until she feared
she had lost her. Her heart still flut-
tered at the thought that Maggie could
have died out there in the woods.

Somehow the afternoon's escapade
put everything into perspective. Nothing mattered but the fact that Maggie
was safe. And now Katherine could let
the house go. If Montgomery Page would
agree to that plan Jake had outlined,
she would take his money and let him
and his daughter have the house. She
would save the money for Maggie's college education.

Yes, she could let the house go. Now

she could go back to her dental office
and forget that she had ever heard of a
log house or Glen St. John.

And Jake? Could she let Jake go?

Katherine sighed, then muttered,
"I'm an idiot! Jake's not mine. He never
was. He's Victoria's."

The tears that crept down Katherine's cheek were salty. She wiped them
away on a corner of the sheet.

It was not fair. There was nothing
fair about it. Victoria would have the
house and Jake. Katherine would have
only the money that the house would
bring. The money would help Maggie,
but...

There was no use in thinking of it.
Life in this paradise was just not for
her, although it would be wonderful.
She belonged in her dental office cleaning teeth and mixing fillings. She realized that.

And yet she could not bear to give up
Jake! She could not!

NINE

Katherine was awakened by thunder very early the next morning. She got up to close her three windows, then went back to bed.

When she awoke a second time, the rain had stopped. She showered, put on clean jeans and a fresh plaid top, and went downstairs, letting Maggie sleep.

The rain had started again and was streaming down the windows.

"It's really coming down, isn't it, Miss Lizzie?"

"Yes, but it's about over." Miss Lizzie

115

put a stack of pancakes on Katherine's plate and added small link sausages.

"About over? Why, it's raining cats and dogs, and look how dark it is!"

"Won't last much longer. The sun's about ready to break through the clouds, and it'll be a nice day for whatever you want to do."

Katherine thought that Miss Lizzie had to be wrong, but she wasn't. In a little more than ten minutes the rain stopped and the sun broke through. April was smiling again.

Warmed by the sun and the tasty breakfast, Katherine felt her spirits lift. She was contentedly sipping her coffee when the telephone rang.

Miss Lizzie went to answer it and came back to say that it was Jake. He wanted to talk to Katherine.

"Hello." It was the familiar drawl which, for some reason, came out more strongly over the telephone wire.

"Did it rain up there on your mountaintop?"

"Yes, it did. It just poured and I thought it would last all day," Katherine said.

"Oh, no. If you look out, you can see there isn't a cloud left in the sky."

He wanted to tell her, he said, that he had tickets for the little theater show tomorrow and had made reservations for dinner at the restaurant called The Dome.

"Fine!" Katherine said. "I'm sure I'll love every minute of it!"

"And tell Maggie I'll pick her up by one o'clock today. We want you to go to the mine with us this time, Katherine."

"All right, I'll go."

She did not really want to go digging for gems, but she should be agreeable, she told herself, knowing all the while that she would like to go anywhere with Jake.

"And another thing, Katherine. Victoria wants to go along."

Her heart fell and she swallowed a gasp. She assumed they were to take

Victoria to dinner and the theater with them.

"Isn't that all right?" Jake asked.

"Why, yes, of course. She'll enjoy the musical," she managed to say.

"I don't mean the theater. I mean Victoria wants to go to the mine with us. It's okay, isn't it?"

"Yes, it's okay." Katherine tried not to show the relief she felt. "I'll tell Maggie, Jake, and we'll be ready by one o'clock."

"And don't forget to wear your old clothes and take a sweater because it can get cool in the mine."

Katherine went back to the kitchen and asked:

"Do you ever go hunting for gems, Miss Lizzie?"

"Not anymore. I used to."

"Did you ever find anything?"

"No, but my youngest son found a nice sapphire. He had it made into a ring for his wife. It's been a good many years, though, since there has been a big find in the mines."

"Then it's not just tourist bait? There are gems?"

"Gracious, yes. There have been some fine things found."

"Well, I'll go and dig, but I'm not being fooled. I know I won't find anything."

TEN

Jake and Victoria came together, and Victoria looked slim and lovely, as usual.

Katherine and Maggie got in the back seat of the car while Victoria sat close to Jake in front. As they drove, Jake and Maggie vied with one another in telling Katherine what it would be like.

"It's fun because you think every minute that you'll find something the next minute," Maggie said.

"It's all a matter of luck," Jake admitted. "Some people find valuable bits, but most don't. Of course, it pays to have sharp eyes."

Maggie said, "I've got sharp eyes and

I'm not as tall as the rest of you. I'm closer to the ground. Besides, I know more now about what to look for and I won't spend my time picking out things that aren't any good. I bet I find something good today."

"Miss Lizzie would tell you not to count your chickens before they're hatched," Katherine warned her.

"Rubies," Jake said, "are always red, but sapphires can be any color."

"I've never found anything," Victoria said. "And, as I tell Jake, I think it's all a hoax and a lot of hanky-panky just to get the tourist money. Of course, he won't agree."

She had been quite gracious since they started, but Katherine sensed the tension under the surface.

"Of course, I won't agree." Jake was emphatic. "Stones have been found around here. I've found several ordinary sapphires, but I never found anything very valuable."

"If I'm going to dig," Victoria said,

"I'd rather find one of the rarer things, the ones that are worth something."

"We should take Sally Jo and let her dig," Maggie said. "She loves to dig holes."

Jake said he had never thought of that, but he did not suppose that Mr. Saltern, the manager, would allow a dog in his Starlite mine.

Less than an hour later, armed with short-handled spades and picks, they walked down the long, cool ramp into the ruby mine.

The mine proper was about twenty by fifty feet and was lighted by naked bulbs. Pails and screens awaited them, and they went to work at once, digging, shoveling, sifting. Half a dozen others were in the mine and there was much laughing, joking, and talking back and forth. An elderly man from Atlanta promised Maggie that if he found a sapphire with ruby stripes, he would give it to her.

For almost two hours they dug and

sifted and picked out bits and pieces only to toss them aside again. Maggie finally put down her shovel and went to work with her hands.

Katherine was not taking her digging too seriously and did not have the vim and pep that the others had. She did not doubt that valuable gems had once been found here, but for the most part she thought that the mines might now just be another trick to trap the tourist dollars. She was surprised when Jake came across to her and asked her what she had in her hand.

She looked at the lump of ore she had picked out of a bucket of sand. It was about the size and the shape of a pecan.

"Oh, it's nothing," she said.

He squinted and looked closer.

"Hit it with your spade."

"Why?"

"See if it breaks."

She hit the lump with the back of her spade, but it did not break.

"Hit it harder."

She hit it as hard as she could. "Why do you want me to break it, Jake?"

Putting down his pail and shovel, he gave the lump a big blow. It did not break.

"Look, Katherine, you could have something."

She stared at him. "You mean that brown rock could be valuable?"

"It's one hard piece of rock." He kept turning it over in his hand while Victoria and Maggie looked over his shoulder, and the other diggers came to look, too.

"You've got to be kidding," Victoria said. "That couldn't be valuable. I would have thrown it out."

"I'm not kidding," he said.

Mr. Saltern, the mine manager, came into the mine and Jake called him over.

Turning the piece of ore around in his hand, the manager whistled and turned to Maggie.

"Who found this? Did you? Kids are always lucky."

Maggie shook her head. "I didn't find it. My sister did."

"Well, Conniston, I think you'd better take this to Asheville and get it appraised."

"Then you agree with me that it could be valuable?" Jake asked.

"I would not be surprised to learn that it is an Oriental topaz and there hasn't been one of those found in these mountains for ages."

"Would it be valuable?" Victoria asked quickly.

"Very."

"Meaning it's worth a lot of money?" she persisted.

"Of course. Now remember, young lady," the manager said, "I'm not saying that it is an Oriental topaz. That's the appraiser's job. But if it is, it's worth some thousands."

Some thousands! Katherine's heart jumped into her throat. How casually he had said that! She thought of what she could do with a few thousand and then she caught herself quickly. She would not allow herself to think that it could be valuable because it was sure to be worthless. Miracles like that did not happen to her.

The manager had come to announce that the mine would close in twenty minutes.

"We'll have to go," Jake said and handed the piece of ore back to Katherine. She dropped it into the needle-point tote bag that held her wallet and sweater.

Back up the cool, damp ramp they walked and returned their spades and picks to the office. Then they went to the wash room to wash.

"You two can go first," Maggie said generously. "I'm more used to being dirty than you are." Her brown eyes surveyed Victoria, who seemed immaculate, but Katherine's hands were dirty.

They put down their bags and sweaters on the table and cleaned up as best they could. Maggie's face was even dirty and Katherine had to have her wash twice.

"I'll go on," Victoria said, "and meet you outside." Taking her purse and sweater, she went out while Katherine combed Maggie's hair.

Half an hour later, they climbed the mountain and drew up in front of the log house.

"I won't come in," Victoria said.

"Oh, yes, come on in a while," Jake ordered her.

"You go ahead. I'll wait here for you." He took Victoria's hand and pulled her out of the car.

"Miss Lizzie might get her feelings hurt if you don't come in," he said, and she came reluctantly. "You know you should say hello at least."

The housekeeper and the dog were waiting for them.

"Well, did you find anything?" Miss Lizzie asked Maggie.

"I didn't, but Kick did."

At that moment Sally Jo jumped on

Victoria and knocked her purse from her hand. The contents scattered in all directions.

"Oh, my heaven!" Victoria exclaimed and actually turned pale, then sank down in a chair.

"Don't worry, Victoria, we'll pick it all up for you." Maggie went down on her hands and knees and began to retrieve lipstick, compact, pencils, tissue pack, and other items that had scattered in all directions.

"There, that's everything," Jake said in a comforting voice. "There was nothing to get excited about now, was there?"

Victoria smiled wanly. "It's just—just that I hate for that to happen. It's like getting undressed in public."

"Don't be ridiculous," Jake said.

"It happens to all of us, Victoria," Katherine told her. "We never know how much we carry in our purses until they get opened and spill everything. Don't worry about it."

Sally Jo, who was scolded and called

a bad girl by Miss Lizzie for jumping up on people, retired to her corner behind the green chair.

Victoria got up and went toward the door.

"Let's go, Jake. I want to go home."

"Wait a minute," Jake said a little impatiently. "We just got here. I want Miss Lizzie to see what Katherine found."

"Show it to Miss Lizzie, Kick," Maggie said.

"Yes, of course." Katherine took her needlepoint tote bag from the old piano where she had put it, then reached in to get the piece of ore. Searching and running her fingers into the corners of the bag, she could not find it. The piece of ore was gone!

With her hand over her mouth, her eyes wide in surprise and consternation, she gasped:

"I've lost it! It's not here! Oh, I shouldn't have carried it in an open bag like that!"

ELEVEN

At Katherine's announcement that
the ore was gone, Jake was silent for a
moment and then held out his hand.

"Here, let me look."

She handed over the bag and he
turned out the contents on the piano.
There was no chunk of ore.

"It could have fallen out when I got
out of the car," Katherine said.

"I'll go look."

They all went out to the car, but it
was not to be found.

Katherine smiled a little bitterly. "I didn't really believe that it was valuable, but I would have liked to have it appraised. Now I'll never know. I wish I hadn't lost it."

Maggie was crying. "It was worth thousands of dollars, Kick, and you lost it!"

"Now, Maggie." Katherine frowned. "We don't know that it was worth anything at all."

Although she tried to put on an indifferent face, she was as disappointed as Maggie and Jake. Victoria only shook her head and said that it was simply too bad.

"I'll go back to the mine and retrace your steps, Katherine," Jake said.

"But the mine will be closed, Jake."

"Yes, but I know where Mr. Saltern lives and he will open up and help me look. Come on, Victoria, I'll take you home. After I've had a good look, I'll come back and let you know, Katherine."

After they had left, Katherine explained the whole thing to Miss Lizzie, who said she was a little confused about it all.

The dog came out from her corner, wanting to be reassured after her scolding, and nuzzled Maggie, who petted her and sobbed at the same time. "Oh, Sally Jo, we thought Kick had found an Oriental topaz and we were going to be rich and now we've—we've lost it!"

"There, there, honey, don't cry about it. Maybe Jake will find it," Miss Lizzie comforted.

"You're letting your imagination run away with you, Maggie. We didn't really believe we'd be rich, you know," Katherine said.

After a while, Miss Lizzie said that it was time to eat and to feed Sally Jo. Katherine said they would wait for Jake.

"I've left chops and potatoes and string beans and corn bread in the oven for you," Miss Lizzie said when she came back from the kitchen in her corduroy jacket and red cap. "There's a blackberry pie you can have. I picked the blackberries myself last summer and this is the last jar I canned. The kettle is hot for tea."

Miss Lizzie had scarcely put the leash on the dog and left when Maggie decided that she was too hungry to wait for Jake. Couldn't they eat now? So Katherine put the food on the table and they were sitting there when Jake returned.

"No luck. We wore out our flashlight batteries and had to quit looking, but I'll go back early tomorrow morning and try again."

"Oh, Jake, why don't we just forget it? It was probably just a worthless rock, and there's no need for you to work so hard to—"

"I don't want to forget it, Katherine." His face looked strained. "You see, I want you to have this place. And if that rock had been an Oriental topaz, you would not have been too stubborn to take money for it. I don't want you to go back to Ohio—I mean, for good. I know you must go back temporarily, but you belong here."

He put his hand over hers and turned to Maggie.

"You know, Maggie, I just love your sister."

Maggie smiled between bites of blackberry pie. "I love her, too, but that's all right." She swallowed some pie and added, "It's all right for you to love her because her heart is big enough for both of us."

Jake looked surprised. "That's right. I think it is."

Katherine filled a plate for him and gave him a cup of hot tea. Maggie sat and solemnly watched him eat.

Finally, she asked in a matter-of-fact tone:

"Did you ever fall in love, Jake?"

He gave a low chuckle. "Well, I thought I did once, but I'm not sure. But you know what? When I find the right girl, I won't fall in love, I'll just parachute straight down to her."

Maggie giggled. "You're funny."

Then, as though they no longer held any interest for her, Maggie said that, if they would excuse her, she would go out and watch for Miss Lizzie and Sally Jo.

"All right," Katherine said, "but don't you get out of sight of this house."

"Now listen, Katherine." Jake put butter on his square of corn bread and took a big bite. "We're not going to let this business of losing the rock spoil our dinner and theater. I may find the thing tomorrow, but if I don't, we're not going to think any more about it."

"That's okay with me."

"You know, I really ought to be glad to see you go back to Ohio because you've been a big worry to me. I'm beginning to wonder what I ever thought about before you arrived."

"Maybe," Katherine said archly, "you thought about Victoria."

His gaze traveled to her lovely eyes.

"You have magic eyes, Katherine, and they keep changing color while one looks at them. I suppose some people might say that they denote a change- able, unreliable character, but I know you well enough to know that isn't so. Right now your eyes are bright with gold lights. They're real hazel eyes, sometimes coppery, sometimes brown, and sometimes almost gold."

She warmed under such close scru- tiny and turned her eyes away. Then she changed the subject.

"You've always lived in the Glen, haven't you, Jake? I think you told me that."

"Nowhere else."

"Don't you ever leave?"

"Oh, yes. I left for college. I've been to Europe. I sometimes go to New York to see some plays and to hear good music. I have a brother in publishing there and a sister who teaches college there."

"But you always want to stay in the Glen?"

"Of course. Do you know a better place?"

"No."

"You see, Katherine, there's been a Judge Conniston here for a long time, so I'm running for circuit court. I'll get it, too. If I ever leave, it will be to go to Washington and sit on the Supreme Court bench. A very remote possibility. But I like to write briefs, and that would suit me."

Although his eyes twinkled as he said it, she thought that he was partly serious. How fine he would look in the long black robe of a Supreme Court Justice!

"But how can you stay in such good physical condition sitting at a lawyer's desk all day?"

Jake looked at her questioningly, as though wondering what kind of a cross examination she was putting him through, and then he laughed.

"Now that's an easy question. It's not hard to stay in good physical condition in the mountains. You have to be tough to live here. Miss Lizzie isn't young, but she's a rugged little pine knot. She can climb these peaks without getting the least bit out of breath."

"Yes, Miss Lizzie told me she could climb the mountain here better than a goat."

"It's perfectly true."

He looked at his watch.

"I must go—a committee meeting. Tell Miss Lizzie I enjoyed the dinner and especially the blackberry pie." He put his hand on Katherine's shoulder and looked straight into her eyes. "Someday I'll take you to pick black-berries and we might see a bear."

When he had gone, she sat turning her teacup about and thinking.

She belonged here—with Jake. He was real, straightforward, kind, loyal—

all those qualities that she admired in a human being.

But, oh, the barriers between them!

Mostly Victoria. Always Victoria.

He had been cagey when he spoke of love. But Katherine knew he loved Victoria. He surely did.

TWELVE

Curtain time was at eight o'clock and Jake would come for Katherine at six. The theater was right next door to the restaurant, so that would save them some time.

Though Katherine wished she had brought something more elegant to North Carolina with her, Maggie and Miss Lizzie told her she looked pretty in her plaid skirt and white blouse.

And when Jake came, he looked at her with frank appreciation, then gave

141

her a quick hug and a kiss on the cheek.

"My, but you look lovely tonight. Like a fresh peach or a shiny apple."

"Just so you don't eat her," Maggie giggled.

He gave the child a reproachful look. "Now that wouldn't make sense, Maggie, because if I ate her, I wouldn't have her anymore."

"No, and we wouldn't either."

"That's right so I promise to return her in good condition."

They waved goodby, got in the car, and the magic evening began.

When they passed the Starlite mine, Jake said that he had gone back and searched but found nothing. Mr. Saltern, however, had promised to keep his eyes open.

"We won't say another word about it tonight, Katherine. Tonight we're going to ignore our problems."

The restaurant was aglow with soft lights from the brass fixtures designed like kerosene lamps on the panelled walls. The table linen was snow white, the leather chairs, dark red, as was the carpet that covered the floor. Lovely music was played by a string quartet, and Katherine was surprised at that.

"I thought it would be country and noisy."

"Oh, no. The Dome is patronized mostly by our own artist colony and by the more artistic summer visitors. They like what they call chamber music."

Katherine felt interested eyes on them as they followed the hostess to their table and Jake nodded to acquaintances, and she knew they looked attractive. But what really made her stomach muscles tighten and her pulses jump was that Jake seemed very proud of her as he drew out the red leather chair.

They ordered wine and made small talk. Soon their dinner came and was delicious: baked veal cutlets, new gar-

den peas with tiny potatoes, fresh broc-
coli, and wild strawberries with thick
cream.

By the time they finished dinner, the
quartet had stopped playing chamber
music and started playing romantic
dance music. They had time for one fast
dance, and it was heavenly. Katherine
just melted in Jake's arms, and she was
sorry they had to leave for the theater.

But the show was enjoyable, too. And
they drove home through the moonlit
night singing or humming the songs
from the musical.

Miss Lizzie had left several lights on
and they shone through the pines and
the hemlocks. Since it was late, Katherine did not invite Jake to come in. He
simply came on his own. Still humming
one of the songs, he threw another log
on the fire and drew Katherine down
to the sofa beside him.

"I don't know about you, but I had a
wonderful time," he said.

"I did too, Jake. I enjoyed every minute—every second of it."

The dog came from her chair to put her paws on Jake's knees. He leaned over and patted her head.

"Now, go lie down, Sally Jo. We're not paying any attention to you or any of our other problems tonight."

The flames leaped up as they sat looking into the fireplace, his arm about her shoulders. They went on talking. Katherine asked about the little theater and how long their season lasted.

"It's all over by September," he said.

"If I didn't have to go home, I'd love to see every performance. Then what do people do in the winter, Jake?"

"We ski and ice skate and there's always hiking. I've hiked all of the Appalachian Trail and done some segments of it in the wintertime. It's more challenging when it's deep in snow."

"And more dangerous too."

"That's right." He smiled. "The thing I like best about you, Katherine, is that you're so understanding. I suppose it's simply a matter of being mature."

She thought of all her uncertainty and her inability to make a decision about the house and of how he had practically told her she had better grow up, but she did not argue the point.

"I've never been accused of being all that mature. What I've been accused of is stubbornness."

He leaned back smiling. "You're stubborn, all right. I've found that out. But to be a little stubborn is not so bad. In court we like to have a witness who will stick to his guns. Do you just have to go back to Ohio on Monday, Katherine?"

He was holding her hand now.

"Yes, Jake, I do. Maggie must be back in school Tuesday and I will have a day filled with appointments."

"Then tomorrow is your last day here. I mean to spend the whole day with you. Now don't tell me no because I won't pay any attention to you."

"I won't tell you no, Jake." Her throat was dry at the thought of the last day.

"I'll come early. By ten. I want to take you for another drive. There are several places I still want to show you. We have some fine falls and other lovely things."

"I'd like that."

"We'll have to talk some more business, too, but no more than necessary."

"All right."

He stood up and drew her to her feet. What Katherine did then was not premeditated for she had no idea she was going to do it until it was done. She put her arms about his neck and kissed him.

"Thank you, Jake, for a perfectly lovely evening."

For a moment he held her close. Then he said good night and left.

Katherine stood still and waited until she could no longer hear his car. Then she put the big screen in front of the fire, turned out the lights, and went up the stairs.

Maggie was sleeping peacefully. She

had spread her rocks on the floor beside
a large poster that had many rocks fastened to it, all labeled in a childish
printing. That was the rock collection
Jake said he had made in the third
grade.

The sight of Jake's collection made
Katherine lose her cool completely and
with it all the common sense she had
always thought she possessed, and she
was crying, sobbing uncontrollably.

It had been a wonderful evening, but
it could never happen again. The thrill
of dancing in his arms, of the way he
kept looking at her, as though she were
one of those gems he was often talking
about—she would never know that
thrill again.

At the thought of what might have
been an Oriental topaz, more tears
came. At least Fate could have let her
keep the gem or whatever it was until
she could find out about it. Instead of
that, she had to lose it.

She went to bed, but she could not

sleep. At two o'clock she got up and went to the bathroom to wash her face. On second thought she put her entire head under the cold-water faucet and let it run until all of her hair was soaked. Feeling better then, she told the red-eyed reflection in the mirror that she had never been a crybaby—and she was going to stop it.

Jake would be there tomorrow—today now—and then it would be goodby.

THIRTEEN

In the morning, as Katherine looked from her window, she saw that April was laughing. Tomorrow she might be raining, but today, their last day in the mountains, April was laughing.

Katherine showered and put on the blue dress. If they were going to explore such things as waterfalls, she supposed that she should wear her jeans, but for some reason she did not want to wear jeans for her last day in the mountains.

Jake wore slacks and his blue sweater.

Maggie had planned to go on the drive with them but changed her mind at the last moment, for Jake had brought her poster paper and a special glue and she wanted to mount her rocks.

"They'll be easier to take home if I have them mounted, Kick, and I want to show Uncle Duval and Aunt Sarah. Jake says I can keep his poster along with mine and show them both to my children when I grow up. I'll take them to school to show the kids, too."

Miss Lizzie warned them to be back from the drive by one o'clock because she was going to have fried chicken for dinner.

From the start, it was a rather quiet drive. Katherine tried to be chatty and cheerful, but it was hard to forget that this was her last drive with Jake. Thanks to the recent rains, the waterfalls were rushing, foaming, and noisy.

They held hands as they gazed down into great valleys or up at high peaks. Jake pointed out the various mountains and told her their names. There were quite a few.

"My goodness, Jake, do you know all of them?"

He nodded. "I think so. Over there." He turned her to the west. "That's Standing Indian. He's everybody's favorite."

"But how can you remember all their names?"

He frowned thoughtfully. "Well, I never thought about it, but I suppose that when you are born and grow up with them, you don't forget their names any more than you forget the names of your friends."

Back at the house, Miss Lizzie had dinner ready for them and Maggie proudly displayed her rock poster.

"See, Jake, I can print better than you could."

"You wouldn't brag, would you, Maggie?" Katherine asked reproachfully, but Jake just smiled and studied the posters.

"Sure enough you can," he agreed.

"Pride goeth before a fall," Miss Liz-

zie warned, and Maggie looked sheep-
ish.

"Well, maybe I can print better, but
you sure knew your rocks, Jake," she
conceded.

Jake turned his head to hide his smile.

They sat at the table talking for a
long time after the delicious dinner and
Jake asked Miss Lizzie if she knew who
had named the mountains.

"No. Can't say that I do. They've all
got names, but they've had them ever
since I can remember."

She and Jake both agreed that the
mountains had personalities and
seemed almost human when you had
grown up with them.

After a while, they all helped to clean
up the kitchen, and Katherine and Jake
went to the living room to sit in front
of the fireplace.

Katherine drew a deep breath. She
knew that the time had come when she
must tell Jake what she wanted him to
do about the house. There was no time

left for vacillating and changing her mind about the matter.

"You're right, Jake;" she began, "if Mr. Page will accept your offer, I think I should take it. It makes no sense for me to sacrifice Maggie's future just because I don't want Victoria to have this house."

He raised an eyebrow.

"It would be selfishness on my part, Jake, because it seems to me that Victoria already has everything."

He put his arm behind her and gently patted her back. "I think you're being smart, Katherine, although I would like you to have the house. It seems to me that you belong here and Victoria doesn't. Still, you should realize something on the deal, and in my opinion, Maggie is definitely college material."

They stopped talking for a while when Miss Lizzie and Maggie put the leash on the dog and went outside. Maggie was objecting to the sweater that Miss Lizzie wanted her to wear, insisting that she wasn't cold, and Katherine had to tell her to put it on.

Jake chuckled. "She's a little stubborn like her sister. Well, I'll get in touch with Mr. Page this week and see what he says about my plan. Of course, he may not consent to the delayed deed and in that case we'll have to start over again, but I think he will agree to it."

"All right."

She sounded cheerful enough, but the truth was that she had not been so downhearted and discouraged since her parents had died.

Maggie and Miss Lizzie came back through the door, bringing in a rush of cool air and making the flames in the fireplace leap higher.

"Sally Jo brought a rock! Look at her!" Maggie cried as she unleashed the dog, who hurried to the corner behind the green chair. Maggie followed and leaned over the back of the chair.

"She's really got a bunch back there now, Miss Lizzie!"

"Yes, I know," Miss Lizzie said, "and I'll just carry them all out right now while I've got my jacket on."

"Oh, do you have to take them away from her?"

"I always leave her two or three, but I can't have her building a rock pile back there, Maggie."

They all laughed a little and Miss Lizzie went to the kitchen and came back with a pail.

"I'll help you," Maggie offered and together they pushed the big chair aside.

"Just hand them to me, Maggie," Miss Lizzie said.

Katherine and Jake paid very little attention to the demolition of Sally Jo's rock collection but sat looking into the fire, deep in thought.

Suddenly, Maggie screamed and they both looked up in alarm.

"Kick! Kick! Look, Kick!" Maggie's scream came down from the high roof like an echo.

Katherine and Jake jumped to their

feet. Maggie was holding up one of the rocks.

"It's the Oriental topaz! Sally Jo had it all the time!"

Astonished, they looked at one another.

"How did she get it?" Katherine demanded.

"Why, she took it out of your bag, Kick."

"That's impossible. I put that tote bag on the piano when I came back, and I didn't move it until I started looking for the rock. The dog certainly did not get up on the piano."

"I don't know. She's very good at sniffing out rocks. Anyway, it's here and you can get it—what's that word?"

"Appraised."

"Yes, I'm sure it's valuable, Kick." Maggie was all but dancing with excitement.

"Let me see it." Miss Lizzie held out a weathered brown hand.

She examined the stone carefully,

running her thumbnail across it. She smiled and her face was like a sunburst.

"You know, I believe you've got something good. The Kingsley company over in Asheville will know in a minute, though, and will tell you all about it." She handed it to Katherine. "It's a mercy the dog didn't swallow it. She could have."

"Oh, no!" Maggie exclaimed. "That would have been awful!"

Jake was not saying a word as the rock was passed around and admired but simply stood looking thoughtful, his eyes lowered.

"Where will I put it, Jake, where the dog won't get it?" Katherine asked.

"I'll take it." He put the stone in his pocket and held out his hand to Katherine.

"Let's take a walk around and look at the flowers," he said.

She sensed that he wanted to talk privately and put her hand in his. They crossed the terrace and went out to his car where he opened the door and took a small canvas bag from the glove compartment. Slipping the stone inside the bag, he drew the drawstring tightly, replaced it in the glove compartment, and then took out his key and locked the compartment.

"The dog won't get it there, but it's not the dog I'm concerned about, Katherine."

"What *are* you concerned about, Jake?" She was feeling relieved, just as though a whole new dimension of time and space and opportunity had opened before her and she could not understand his evident worry.

He did not answer immediately but took a tighter grip on her hand as they walked down to the little bridge and stood looking down at the water tumbling over the stones.

"You can't go home now, Katherine," he said. "You'll have to wait until we get the appraisal."

She shook her head. "I've got to go,

Jake. I've got my work and Maggie has to go to school. My uncle has been very good to me, but I couldn't ask him for more time."

Their eyes met and hers were unswerving and stubborn while his gaze was puzzled and thoughtful.

"Won't you take care of the stone for me, please, Jake? I know it's asking you to spend your time for something that may prove to be worthless, but if you would—"

"I'm tied up in court tomorrow and Tuesday. It would be Wednesday before I could go to Asheville."

"Well, isn't that all right?"

The uncertainty in his eyes disturbed her. She could not understand why he should be so worried now that the stone had been found.

"If you want to trust it to me, I'll take care of it as soon as I can," he promised.

"Why, of course, I'll trust it to you."

"There are other things, too, you know."

"You're thinking of Mr. Page?"

"Yes, but let's not talk any more about it—just let the whole thing simmer. I'll soon need to get back to the office and prepare for some arguments tomorrow. We don't have much time left, Katherine, so let's not waste it."

His arm slipped round her waist. Standing there against the warmth of his nearness, she felt a surge of happiness that she had never known before. Could it be?—was it possible?—oh, no! She must be sensible. He was her lawyer and he was just being kind. All of this would end soon and he would forget her.

But why was Jake so grim? Had she done something or said something to offend him?

They left the bridge and walked along a path, carpeted with pine needles, through the laurel. Talking little, they paused to listen to a cardinal calling insistently, or to watch a pair of squirrels scampering away somewhere.

The path was leading to a clearing in the thick laurel and Katherine was surprised to see a plot of ground enclosed by a low iron fence.

"What is this?" she asked and unconsciously lowered her voice.

"The pet cemetery."

"Yes, of course." She had never even wondered what had become of all the dogs her grandmother had owned through the years.

The plot was rather large and it was well kept, but there were no real markers or tombstones. Each grave had a white brick with a name in block letters on it. That was all. Katherine lifted her surprised face.

"I know what you're thinking," he said. "It's hard to understand your grandmother's feeling for all those dogs, but she was not sentimental about them and would never dream of putting up tombstones and epitaphs as some people do, even for her favorites. She had a reverence for all life and told me once that taking care of stray dogs was something that she *could* do."

The path ended and they returned to the bridge the way they had come.

Katherine could think of nothing to say, but she was glad she had seen that pet cemetery. She would never feel hatred or even dislike for her grandmother again.

"That was—impressive," she said finally.

He nodded indifferently, probably because he had seen the pet cemetery often through the years.

"Katherine," he said, "I won't see you any more before you leave, but I'll keep in touch."

This was goodby then, their private goodby.

"I want to thank you, Jake, for being so kind to me and especially to Maggie. She'll never forget you."

"Will you forget me?"

Again, before Katherine knew it, her arms were about his neck.

"Never, Jake, never."

He held her close, then loosened her arms and took her hand.

"Let's go inside, Katherine. I know where you live in Ohio and I have your telephone number. I'll keep in touch."

This was goodby. She would not be alone with him again.

FOURTEEN

It was Friday again and near the end of April. Rain had started in the night when the crescent moon had retreated behind the banks of clouds. It was still coming down.

But the rain had not kept the tough old senator from his dental appointment.

"Now, if you will, Senator, just hold the film on the roof of your mouth with your tongue. There, that's fine." Katherine gave him a bright smile although,

167

swathed in his white cloth and with his eyes closed, the old man did not see it.

She went on talking in a cheerful voice. "This will be the last picture, Senator, and I'll bet a dollar to a jelly doughnut that your teeth will check out fine."

Then switch on, switch off, and back to the developing room. Then out again—and she was sounding the buzzer for Uncle Duval to come and check the X-ray pictures with her.

Just as she predicted, the pictures showed good teeth and the senator did not need any work done. Katherine helped him out of the chair and into his jacket.

The old man was a health enthusiast and seldom left the office without reading them a little lecture.

"You see, Sam, you and Katherine ought to tell your patients to stop using all those sweet-flavored toothpastes on their teeth. If they would use only salt and soda as I do, they would not have cavities or gum problems."

They always listened to him with re-
spect for, after all, he was eighty years
old and his theories, or at least something, were surely working for him.

Uncle Duval said he looked younger,
instead of older, every time he came
and he would surely go to a hundred.
The senator himself said he was shoot-
ing for a hundred and twenty.

Katherine thought of Sally Jo as she
put away her instruments. She was
through now until Monday and she was
in a hurry to get back to the apartment
and see if there was a letter from Jake.
The last thing he had said to her was
that she would be hearing from him,
and she thought that he would call, but
there had not been a word.

Had something gone wrong? Was Mr.
Page refusing to agree to that advance
contract that Jake had in mind? And
what about his plan to take the stone
to the appraiser at Asheville?

Maggie, sensing her restlessness,

asked Katherine why she did not call Jake, but Katherine shook her head.

"No. He said he would keep in touch."

Putting on her raincoat, she drew the belt snugly about her trim waist and looped it, picked up her purse, went out, and closed the door.

She was halfway down the passage to the open counter when she heard the secretary's voice.

"I'm sorry, sir, but office hours are over. I won't be able to give you an appointment before next Tuesday."

A familiar drawl made Katherine's heart jump into her throat.

" I don't want an appointment, ma'am. I want to see Miss Lonsdale."

"Jake!" Katherine cried and ran toward him. He looked up and in another minute they were in one another's arms.

The secretary looked puzzled, shrugged, and then smiled.

"Katherine, have you been keeping something from us?" she asked.

Katherine unwrapped herself from Jake's long arms.

"Oh, I'm sorry, Cleo. This is Mr. Conniston. He is from Glen St. John where Maggie and I were last week, you know."

"How do you do," Cleo said primly.

The dentist came to the counter and handed her some files. He looked over his glasses at Katherine and Jake, no longer embracing but still holding hands.

"Uncle Duval, this is Jake Conniston from the Glen. You know, you talked to him on the phone."

Katherine knew she was being rather awkward and not at all gracious, but she couldn't seem to recover from her surprise at Jake's coming *here*.

"You didn't tell us he was coming, Katherine."

"I didn't know it," Katherine said as the men shook hands.

Great as Katherine's surprise at

seeing Jake had been, it was mild compared with Maggie's. She was a whirlwind of delight and demanded to know about Sally Jo and Miss Lizzie as though she had been gone a year instead of a week.

"Everybody's fine," Jake said, and then, turning to Katherine, added, "My secretary, Sondra Lonsdale, said to tell you to hurry back to the Glen because you and she had a lot to talk about."

"Did you get the rock appraised?" Maggie asked anxiously.

Katherine held her breath and waited for his answer.

"Yes, I did."

"And it was good and we're rich, aren't we?" Maggie said.

Jake laughed and shook his head. "Now, let's don't jump to conclusions, honey. Let's just say we are considering offers on the stone."

Katherine realized that Jake did not want to talk about the Glen much with

Maggie, so she did not ask questions.

He glanced about the living room of the apartment. The three of them seemed to fill it.

"And this is where you answered my telephone call?" he asked.

She nodded.

That gave Maggie an idea. "Kick, can't we have hamburgers and fries and shakes tonight? It's really a celebration with Jake here."

"I guess so," Katherine agreed.

It was much later, after Maggie had gone to bed, before Katherine really learned anything about what had taken place after she left the Glen.

The rain was still coming down—not in a deluge, but steadily. Katherine struck a match to the little gas grate.

"It's not like having logs to watch, but it takes off the chill."

Jake was occupying the big chair and stretched out his legs. "It's fine. Quite cozy. I didn't call you, Katherine, because I wanted to keep your identity secret and I couldn't trust telephone operators."

He held up his hand when she started to ask why.

"No, let me talk first and then ask your questions. To begin with, I've said nothing at all to Mr. Page about the house and you'll understand why later. I went to the appraiser on Wednesday. Kingsley called two consultants. The stone is an Oriental topaz, all right, and very valuable."

Katherine swallowed hard. He did not need to worry about her asking questions because at the moment she could not have spoken.

"Reporters have been hounding me all week and they would have hounded you had I not refused to say who found the stone. They only know that a woman from out of the state found it. Our best offer so far is for sixty-five thousand. Kingsley says to hold out for a hundred thousand."

"A hundred thousand!" It was incredible that such an ugly little rock could be worth that much money! And just to think that the dog had added it to her "rock pile"!

"But, Jake," she said finally, "other people know that I found the rock."

"Yes, I know, but Miss Lizzie and Sondra Lonsdale can be trusted to keep quiet."

"But Victoria knows."

"Yes, I'm coming to that. Do you remember how upset Victoria was when the dog jumped up on her and spilled the contents of her purse?"

"Well, yes, but—"

"And you weren't at all suspicious?"

"Suspicious? Suspicious of what, Jake?"

He looked at her closely and then shook his head slowly and leaned over to take her hand.

"Well, perhaps you wouldn't be but I had seen the same thing happen before and Victoria only laughed. I was suspicious. After the stone was found, I told her I knew what she had done. She confessed then that she had taken the rock from your bag just before she left the wash room while you were combing Maggie's hair. It was in her purse and when the contents of her purse spilled over the floor, the dog found the rock and hid it."

"Why, Jake!" Katherine was speechless.

She watched his face because it had grown so very stern. She knew then that anger would run silent and deep in Jake Conniston.

"I put it to her straight. It was plain larceny—grand larceny, to be exact—and if you preferred charges against her, she could go to prison for a good long stay. Of course, Katherine, I knew that you would never send Victoria to prison, but I thought it would be good for her to sweat a little. She kept crying and saying that she didn't want the stone. She just didn't want you to get enough money to keep the house. Now listen, Kath—"

He stopped abruptly because two tears had come rolling down Katherine's cheeks. "Now why are *you* crying?"

"But, Jake, I feel sorry for her. I know what it's like to—"

"Well, don't. Don't feel sorry for her. I don't. I thought I cared about her once. How wrong I was! I told her straight out that I had an awfully low opinion of her!"

"I—I think you were too hard on her, Jake."

He did not answer but reached over and wiped the tears away with his finger.

"If I was too hard on her, it was only because I knew what she would have done to you if she could. She's gone now. Her father told Miss Lizzie that his daughter was on the verge of a nervous breakdown and he was taking her back to Miami. The house will be yours, Katherine."

"Yes, I know, and I am glad, Jake." Was it always this way? she wondered. Was real joy always tempered by a little sadness?

"There are a great many decisions to make, but I have made the important one," he said.

"You have?"

"Yes." He sat on the arm of her chair. "I have decided that I want to marry you. I came up here to ask your uncle for his permission — not that I wouldn't have married you without it, but I'm an old-fashioned man and I believe in tradition."

"Now wait a minute." She was on the defensive. He was just a little too sure of himself. "Before you talk to my uncle, it might be a good plan to ask me. If you believe in tradition, you should know that it's customary to ask the girl."

"Oh, I've done that and she's told me. I know she loves me and wants to marry me."

At her look of surprise he gave his low chuckle.

"It's true that the evidence is circumstantial but it's more convincing than direct evidence in this case. Your eyes told me, Katherine, and eyes can't be forced to lie. Now, are there any objections? If there are, they'll be overruled."

"No objections," she whispered, turning her face for his wondrous kiss.